TODAY'S WRITERS
AND THEIR WORKS

ABRAHAM RODRIGUEZ

Cavendish Square
New York

TODAY'S WRITERS
AND THEIR WORKS

ABRAHAM RODRIGUEZ

Richard Andersen

Rogers High School
MEDIA CENTER
Rogers, MN 55374

Cavendish Square

New York

Once again and for always: Diane

With acknowledgement and appreciation for the help I received from
Anna Greene, Yahira Semprit, Michelle Bisson, and Diane Lyn.
With special gratitude to Fernando Gonzalez de Leon, professor of history at Springfield
College in Massachusetts, for his expert review of this manuscript.

Published in 2014 by Cavendish Square Publishing, LLC
303 Park Avenue South, Suite 1247, New York, NY 10010
Copyright © 2014 by Cavendish Square Publishing, LLC
First Edition
No part of this publication may be reproduced, stored in a retrieval system, or transmitted in any form or by any means—electronic, mechanical, photocopying, recording, or otherwise—without the prior permission of the copyright owner. Request for permission should be addressed to Permissions, Cavendish Square Publishing, 303 Park Avenue South, Suite 1247, New York, NY 10010. Tel (877) 980-4450; fax (877) 980-4454.

Website: cavendishsq.com

This publication represents the opinions and views of the author based on his or her personal experience, knowledge, and research. The information in this book serves as a general guide only. The author and publisher have used their best efforts in preparing this book and disclaim liability rising directly or indirectly from the use and application of this book.

CPSIA Compliance Information: Batch #WS13CSQ

All websites were available and accurate when this book was sent to press.

Library of Congress Cataloging-in-Publication Data
Andersen, Richard, 1946–
Abraham Rodriguez / Richard Andersen. • p. cm.—(Today's writers and their works)
Includes bibliographical references and index. • Summary: "Explores the life, work, and themes of author Abraham Rodriguez"—Provided by publisher.
ISBN 978-1-62712-153-8 (hardcover) ISBN 978-1-62712-147-7 (paperback)
ISBN 978-1-60870-762-1 (ebook)
1. Rodriguez, Abraham, 1961–Juvenile literature. 2. Puerto Ricans in literature—Juvenile literature. I. Title. • PS3568.O34876Z54 2012 • 813'.54—dc22• 2010047196

Art Director: Anahid Hamparian
Series Designer: Alicia Mikles. • Photo research by Lindsay Aveilhe

The photographs in this book are used by permission and through the courtesy of:
Daily News L. P: cover photo; Akashic Books © 2008 Abraham Rodriguez: p. 8; Russ åEngel/101St Airborne/Time Life Pictures/Getty Images: p. 12; Orlando/Getty Images: p. 20; JP Laffront/Sygma/Corbis: p. 24; AP Photo/Lynne Sladky: p. 30; Granger Collection: p. 33; Keystone Features/Getty Images: p. 36; Alex Farnsworth/The Image Works: p. 39; Milkweed Editions © 1992: Cover painting by R.W. Scholes: p. 42; Robert Brenner/PhotoEdit: p. 45; AP Photo: p. 48; Mel Rosenthal/The Image Works: p. 52; Marc Romanelli/Getty Images: p. 56; AP Photo: p. 67; Courtesy of Vintage Espanol, a division of Random House, Inc., New York. Copyright of the translation © 1998 Random House, Inc.: p. 72; Masterfile: p. 75; Somos Images/Alamy: p. 80; The Granger Collection: p. 95; John Springer Collection/Corbis: p. 98; Copyright © 2001 by Abraham Rodriguez. Courtesy of Picador USA: p. 108; Courtesy of Akashic Books © 2008 Abraham Rodriguez: p. 114; Everett Collection: p. 117; Joseph Rodriguez/Black Star/Newscom: p. 120.

Printed in the United States of America

CONTENTS

Introduction	9
1. Life and Times	13
2. How the South Bronx Became El Bronx	29
3. "The Boy Without a Flag" and Other Stories	43
4. *Spidertown: A Novel* and "Baptism Under Fire"	73
5. *The Buddha Book: A Novel* and *South by South Bronx*	109
Chronology	122
Works	124
Notes	126
Further Information	127
Bibliography	128
Index	137

There is no cultural document that is not at the same time a record of barbarism.
 —Walter Benjamin

FICTION • A TRADE PAPERBACK ORIGINAL

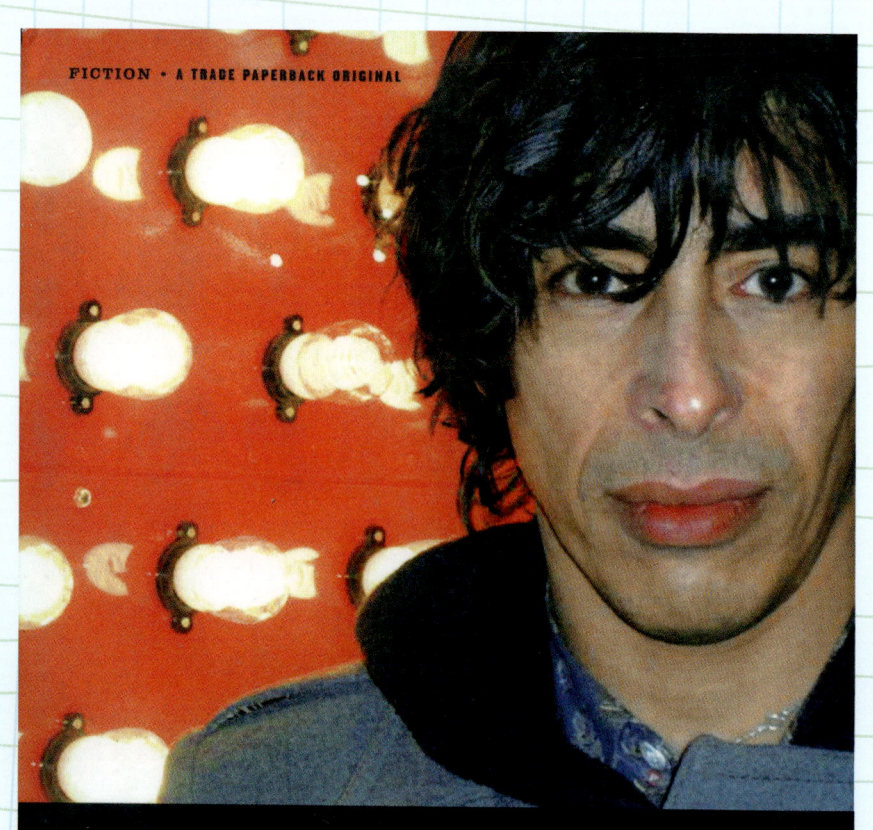

"In prose entirely his own (and don't I wish I could steal it and run off with it!), Abraham Rodriguez gives us a crime story, a love story, and one of the best portraits of the creative process I've ever seen. Every page is a joy and every character—including the South Bronx itself—is alive and surprising. This book is something special."

—**S.J. ROZAN**, Edgar Award–winning author of *In This Rain*

Abraham Rodriguez has maintained his focus on the have-nots of the world throughout his two-decades-long career as a fiction writer.

INTRODUCTION

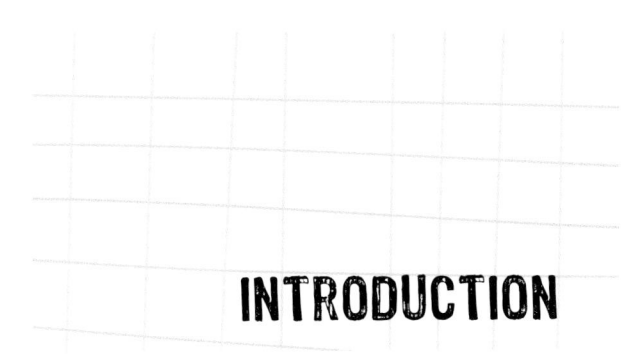

Book love is holier than nations and flags, and knows no culture. It crosses boundaries and opens up the world to a mind, young or old.
—Abraham Rodriguez

ABRAHAM RODRIGUEZ established his reputation as an important Latino writer when his short story collection, *The Boy Without a Flag*, made the *New York Times* Ten Most Notable Books list of 1993. Critics praised his portrayal of Puerto Rican teenagers coming of age in an urban community racked by poverty, drugs, and violence. They also noted his ability to record accurately on paper the spellings, sounds, and cadences of English as it is spoken in New York's South Bronx. Rodriguez's short stories have since appeared in anthologies of Latino, Puerto Rican, and American literature.

Rodriguez solidified his reputation as an impassioned, aggressively honest narrator of the plight of young people in the South Bronx with the publication of his first novel,

Spidertown, in 1992. The book has been translated into Dutch, German, and Spanish, published in a British edition, optioned for a film by Columbia Pictures, and honored with a 1995 American Book Award.

Many of the characters appearing in Rodriguez's short stories show up in the novel, and though the plots vary, the author maintains throughout them all his focus on people caught in the web of an illegal drug economy. Mostly ignorant of the larger societal forces that shape their world, these characters see few options beyond the community they refer to as *El Bronx*. Rodriguez's depiction of this bleak island of brick and cement also frames his outspoken criticism of an older generation of Puerto Rican writers whose portrayals of New York after World War II are, in his view, no longer relevant: "I've never read any books written by Latinos that talked about the life I was experiencing."

Perhaps because of his outspoken criticism of writers such as Piri Thomas and Miguel Piñero, whose works are part of a a tradition that narrates the continuing experience of Puerto Ricans living on the mainland, Rodriguez has been ignored by many Puerto Rican writers whose works appear in English. Few academics have mentioned his works, and much of the treatment is negative, accusing him of exploiting and perpetuating Puerto Rican stereotypes through his use of harsh street language and the characters—mostly junkies, drug dealers, pregnant teenagers, and irresponsible young fathers—who speak it. However others, such as Juan Flores, argue the opposite. *Abraham Rodriguez* is the first book-length examination of Rodriguez's works.

Introduction

In his second novel, *The Buddha Book*, which was published in 2001, Rodriguez reframed the structure he used in *Spidertown* to create a more pessimistic ending. This did nothing to diminish either his wide readership or his high-profile status as an opinionated chronicler of Puerto Ricans living in New York City, people whom Rodriguez and other writers often refer to as *Nuyoricans*, a term that blends the American-Spanish word for New Yorkers, *nuyorquino*, and Puerto Rican. His departure from traditional narrative forms to the multiple-perspective telling of *South by South Bronx,* his latest novel to date, which was published in 2008, did not alienate his readerships either.

Whether Rodriguez will maintain his relentlessly unromantic view of El Bronx or direct his energies more toward those who have risen above their circumstances and celebrate the cultural diversity that has become a focus for many contemporary Puerto Rican writers, musicians, and artists remains to be seen. For now, he seems dedicated to providing a voice for those disenfranchised Nuyoricans whose lives have been damaged by poverty, drugs, and racism, and to serving as a model for those who seek through imaginative forms of self-expression a way out of communities whose names have become synonymous with urban blight.

As a boy, Abraham Rodriguez became an expert on World War II. He would have been familiar with the background of the Battle of the Bulge, and the devastation that resulted from it.

LIFE AND TIMES

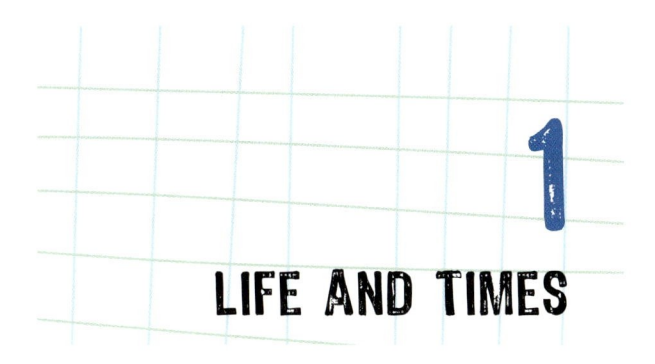

> You write about what you know. I've lived in the South Bronx all my life. I've known a lot of young people who lived this kind of life and I've never seen it written.
>
> —Abraham Rodriguez

Rodriguez's "Jewish" Heritage

Abraham Rodriguez was born to Puerto Rican parents in 1961, but the kids in his predominantly Puerto Rican neighborhood often teased him by saying he was Jewish. They said his first name came from the Bible and his nose was big. Relying on stereotypes of people they had little contact with, they also pointed out that Rodriguez waved his hands too much when he talked.

Rodriguez knew he wasn't Jewish. However, he became interested in Jewish history and began reading about it at an early age. He was especially concerned and frightened by the Holocaust, which took place during World War II, and even had nightmares about the Gestapo arresting him in his home in the South Bronx and shipping him to a death camp in Europe. Like the narrator in his short story "The Boy Without a Flag," Rodriguez read William Shirer's massive *The Rise and Fall of the Third Reich* while he was still in junior high school. The short story that won him his first fiction competition in college wasn't about Puerto Ricans living in the South Bronx but a German soldier befriending a dog on the Eastern Front. He is married to a woman from Germany with whom he lives in Berlin.

Rodriguez sees some important parallels between the conditions of Nuyoricans living in El Bronx—the setting for almost all of his stories—and many of the Jews who lived in Germany and other parts of Europe before World War II: they are restricted to a ghetto, they are mostly poor, and they are given few opportunities for advancement. And that, according to Rodriguez, is how the dominant white culture wants to keep them. In *Puerto Rican Voices in English: Interviews with Writers*, he tells us, "It's not just something that happens; it's a system of control, and the more you're out there, the more you see what's happening, the more you realize that's what it is. It's a system of control and it works perfectly."

The "lowercase people"

For Rodriguez, the impoverished, disenfranchised people who live in the South Bronx don't just happen to be Puerto Rican. Nor did they just happen to wind up there. Through its agencies in government, business, and education, the dominant culture has used such diverse forms of social control as underperforming schools, institutionalized violence, organized poverty, and a corrupt law-enforcement system to create a huge pool of mostly unskilled workers to compete for menial jobs that don't pay enough to support families. Because there are far fewer of these jobs than people, these forms of oppression have created a culture in which some people despair of achieving success in traditional ways and turn instead to criminal behavior to improve the quality of their lives. Most of Rodriguez's stories are about this subset of Puerto Ricans. He calls them, in the words of Miguel in *Spidertown: A Novel*, the "lowercase people." They don't count for much, and they don't have much going for them.

The place where these people live, the South Bronx, is more than a location on a map. It is a concentration camp of the mind and spirit that Rodriguez writes about with insight and anger. Though much of his anger is directed toward those who control from afar the people and events that take place in El Bronx—the slum landlords with offices on Park Avenue, for example, or the kingpins of international drug cartels who never have to set foot in a barrio—Rodriguez champions the cause of their victims: the bewildered teenagers who desire little more than the normal, everyday trappings of what they think is a conventional American life—the kind they see on television—with little or no sense of the forces that have been arrayed to stop them from achieving it.

Early Years and Influences

Rodriguez's parents moved to the United States mainland in the 1950s, his mother from Fajardo and his father from San Juan. Ambitious, hard working, and determined to provide a better life for the two children they would raise, they settled in a working-class section of the Bronx known as Mott Haven. Suffering from asthma at an early age, Abraham rarely experienced the freedom of hanging out with his schoolmates or playing street games with the other kids on his block. Left to his own devices, he read rather than ran. And instead of getting down to the music of Santana, he turned onto the Beatles.

Perhaps to distract him from what was missing in his son's life and provide the boy with another way to entertain himself, Mr. Rodriguez gave Abraham a manual typewriter when he was ten years old. Abraham had always been fascinated by the clacking sounds his father produced while composing poems. Those sounds are Rodriguez's earliest memory, and the typewriter was the way he and his father had bonded for as far back as he can remember. His favorite experience as a child was sitting on his dad's lap and banging away at the keys. Writing for Rodriguez, then, was at first not so much about telling stories as creating music from the special clacking sounds that come from manual typewriters. They even have a bell, which rings every time a lever is pulled to begin a new line of type.

As an adult, Rodriguez still likes to write his short stories and novels on manual typewriters. He owns at least fourteen of them. One of his favorites has a key—the letter "o"—that strikes the paper so hard it puts little holes in it. The result is a work of art that allows beautiful beams of fragmented light to pass through the paper. Rodriguez attended P.S. 25, the first bilingual public school in New York City, one measurement of the extent to which Spanish

Life and Times

was spoken in his neighborhood. Spanish-speaking students who were not proficient in English took classes in English language acquisition. These students were also instructed in Spanish in core subjects such as literature, history, math, and science so they wouldn't fall behind the English-speaking students. Because he read, wrote, and spoke English at grade levels above those of his peers, Rodriguez was placed in the advanced all-English classes.

Most of the time he was at P.S. 25, however, he was bored. Though mostly well meaning, his teachers were generally uninspired, and the curriculum wasn't challenging. On some subjects—especially World War II—Rodriguez probably knew more than many of the instructors. While still in elementary school, he stole books from the adult section of the public library that he wasn't allowed to check out because of his age. He also wrote his own war novels and science fiction stories, and dreamed of the day he'd publish his own magazines.

What first attracted Rodriguez to reading was comic books. He loved the outsized graphic pictures and the short, hard-hitting sentences of dialogue. He still enjoys reading them, and they play a significant role in his writing. Two of the characters in the short story "The Boy Without a Flag" and two of the characters in *The Buddha Book: A Novel* write, illustrate, print, and distribute their own underground comic books to the students in their schools. Rodriguez has also said that he is looking for a Puerto Rican illustrator to work with him on a graphic novel.

Perhaps hoping to provide their son with the intellectual challenges they feared he wouldn't receive at the high school in their Bronx neighborhood, and to provide him with an opportunity to learn more about his Hispanic culture, Mr. and Mrs. Rodriguez enrolled their son in 1973 at Benjamin Franklin High School in the Spanish Harlem section of Manhattan. Within a year he was using the school's mimeograph machine to publish his own magazines. He gave one of his English teachers a copy of a Star Trek fanzine he'd produced in the hope of receiving approval from a person with some professional authority in the field of literature.

What he got was something very different. Instead of praising Rodriguez, or at least encouraging him to keep writing, the teacher just laughed and told the boy that there was no such thing as a Puerto Rican writer. He then went on to advise Rodriguez not to put himself through the humiliation of trying to become one. He also told the boy to think about working as a plumber or an electrician instead. Rodriguez echoes this sentiment when he has the narrator of his novel *Spidertown* comment, "Puerto Ricans didn't write books. Miguel had never even seen one."

How could Rodriguez not have? His father was an ardent reader and an informed advocate of independence for Puerto Rico. It's hard to believe he didn't pass on or even mention to his bookworm son a work by Piri Thomas, Edwin Torres, "Lefty" Barreto, or Miguel Piñero. The father in "The Boy Without a Flag," who is based on Rodriguez's father, surely did. But Rodriguez has claimed he never heard of these or any other Puerto Rican writers until he was much older. He cites Honoré de Balzac and Leo Tolstoy, great writers who were concerned about social issues, as early influences. And he must know that his works are also part of a long chain of

American social-justice novels that includes Harriet Beecher Stowe's renowned antislavery novel, *Uncle Tom's Cabin* of 1850, and Upton Sinclair's attack on conditions for factory workers at the turn of the century in *The Jungle*. Whatever books written by Puerto Ricans the young Rodriguez may have been exposed to—he mentions Pedro Albizu Campos as an influence as early as junior high school—none spoke to him about the people he knew: the victims of broken families, relentless misogyny, shrinking economies, substandard housing, endemic racism, and widespread drug use.

According to Rodriguez, what was important to the older generation of writers, who could not have foreseen the impact drugs would have on Puerto Rican communities in New York, was the mass migration from Puerto Rico after World War II, seeing snow for the first time, and reimagining Puerto Rico as some kind of lost paradise. What he wanted to read about was the many Nuyoricans such as himself who had been born in New York City and knew little if anything about Puerto Rico. Where were the books about community poverty, teenage pregnancy, crack addiction, and gang violence?

What Rodriguez didn't know at the time was that a Puerto Rican writer who wrote in 1967 about Harlem in *Down These Mean Streets* and with whom he might identify—Piri Thomas—lived only a few blocks from his school. When he found out years later, he became angry at Thomas for not visiting the school and doing more to encourage Puerto Rican children to seek self-expression through the arts.

It is for this and other reasons that, as a young adult, Rodriguez volunteered to participate in a number of writ-

Immigrants from Puerto Rico after World War II lived in the poorest areas of New York.

ing workshops sponsored by the Supportive Children's Advocacy Network in East Harlem. He taught the children that writing is, first and foremost, about expressing yourself, and he often invited them to read and critique his stories. In 2000 he won a grant for writing from the New York Foundation for the Arts and later served on the literary panel for the New York State Council on the Arts. But his interest in children never waned, and he continues to respond with personal letters to those who write to him.

By his second year of high school, Rodriguez was feeling increasingly alienated. He was bored with his school's curriculum, frustrated with being a writer in a community that didn't value writing, and tired of being a long-haired loner who listened to rock when all the other kids were into soul. Rodriguez dropped out of school at the age of sixteen and spent the next few years reading, writing, and learning to play the guitar well enough to start a band of his own. His parents, who had hoped their brilliant son would become a doctor or a lawyer and equated rock and roll with sex and drugs, were very disappointed. Perhaps because they wanted to give him a taste of what the world was like without an education, Mr. and Mrs. Rodriguez insisted that the boy get a job.

And because running drugs wasn't the option in the Rodriguez family that it is for the characters in his books, Rodriguez had to settle for stocking store shelves and the like. During an interview for a job at a jewelry store in the late 1970s, he got to talking with the owner about his experiences in World War II. The man had fought in the Battle of the Bulge—the last major offensive by the German army on the Western Front—and was surprised to discover that Rodriguez knew more about the action that took place in the Ardennes Forest than he did. He couldn't believe the boy had never graduated from high school.

Answering the Wake-Up Call

Inspired by the store owner's response to what he knew about World War II, and encouraged by his sister to see if he had the talent to become a writer whose works were good enough to publish, Rodriguez took the exam for his high school general equivalency diploma (GED) and enrolled in the City College of New York in 1982. He remembers trembling with fear in his first creative writing class. Writing was all he'd ever wanted to do with his life. What if his teacher, a Greek poet named Konstantin Lourdas, thought his work was no good? Would he have to follow his high school teacher's advice and consider becoming a plumber or electrician instead?

Rodriguez's problem, though he didn't know it then, was not his intelligence, talent, or ambition. It was his subject matter. Most of his stories were about Nazi soldiers on the Eastern Front of Europe. And they weren't bad. A story about a German sniper who befriends a dog won Rodriguez his first of two successive awards for creative writing in City College's Goodman Fund Short Story contest. It wasn't until Lourdas introduced him to the Puerto Rican writer Edward Rivera, who became his mentor, that Rodriguez discovered his true subject. Best known for his novel *Family Installments: Memories of Growing Up Hispanic* (1982), Rivera told the budding writer to come home from the Eastern Front and write about what he knew and what no one else was writing about: the South Bronx.

The effect of Rivera's suggestion cannot be overestimated. Rodriguez now not only had a subject, he had a "calling." He wrote, "I could see the loneliness of it now, writing in English while coming from a community that doesn't worship the written word. The everyday challenge of it made every typed word a major victory deserving of a night rally."

In addition to leading Rodriguez to the subject he knew best, Rivera also confirmed the young man's love of books, validated his desire to write, and encouraged him to develop his extraordinary narrative talent. Through his own experiences and those of people he knew, he could give authentic voice to and speak with authority about the everyday lives of inner-city Nuyoricans. Under Rivera's guidance, Rodriguez began to discover and develop his own writing voice—El Bronx.

Realizing he didn't need a college degree to write and eager to answer his calling without the distraction of schoolwork, Rodriguez dropped out in 1985. While developing the narrative voice that characterizes his published fiction, he also devoted more time to writing the songs played by a punk rock band he'd help create in 1983. The band, for which Rodriguez also played the guitar, was called Urgent Fury. Along with two friends from the Puerto Rican community in Brooklyn, he performed in clubs as far away from New York as Chicago. The band even managed to put out a record before it broke up in 1990.

Through it all, Rodriguez kept writing fiction and reading works by authors recommended to him by Rivera: Richard Price, Isaac Babel, Honoré de Balzac, and Piri Thomas. He also learned about a publishing house for Latino writers called Arte Público but was not enthusiastic about the work they produced. The stories they published didn't seem as authentic as the work he was creating on some of the same subjects. When he sent Arte Público one of his own stories, "Babies," he discovered why. The editors changed the voice he created to turn his story into standard English prose. Rodriguez was furious. He wanted his story to read as if it had been written by one of the characters he writes about, namely, the poor, undereducated street kids of El Bronx who haven't gone to the kinds of schools where young people are taught to look, think, and sound like those in the American cultural mainstream.

But editors at other publishing companies had reactions similar to those at Arte Público. Some even considered Rodriguez's use of the "substandard" Nuyorican dialect to

Abraham Rodriguez

In the 1970s, the streets of the Bronx were filled with gangs, among the most famous of which were the Savage Skulls, a Puerto Rican street gang whose trademark was a sleeveless denim jacket with a skull and crossbones design. These were the people the young Abraham Rodriguez would soon depict with such graphic accuracy in his fiction.

be subversive, as if reading his work would lead to teens all over America suddenly speaking Spanglish, shooting heroin, and blasting one another with automatic weapons. A few editors even considered his characters' frank and direct references to sex to be vulgar. Perhaps these editors forgot that classics such as Mark Twain's *Adventures of Huckleberry Finn*, J. D. Salinger's *Catcher in the Rye*, D. H. Lawrence's *Lady Chatterley's Lover*, and James Joyce's *Ulysses* have been similarly banned and vilified through the years because their representations of sexuality and racism are narrated through language that some consider coarse.

What the editors failed to appreciate is that one reason why these classics and many other great works of literature are so memorable is the very same realness of language that they objected to in Rodriguez. He doesn't just tell us about the South Bronx—any sociologist could do that—he puts us right on the worst of its streets. Through the language of Rodriguez's narrators, we don't just see what he's talking about, we hear and feel it. And we feel it so strongly we often get the impression Rodriguez didn't just choose to write these stories; he really was "called," as he says, to record them on paper.

Nevertheless, the rejections from publishers piled up, and it didn't take long for Rodriguez to become discouraged. He kept writing, though, and in 1989 "Babies" was published in *Best Stories from New Writers* from Writer's Digest Books.

Publication!

The book that put Rodriguez on the literary map was his collection of seven short stories *The Boy Without a Flag: Tales of the South Bronx*. The largely autobiographical story from which the book receives its title is about a young boy who, as Rodriguez himself once did, refuses to salute the American flag during an assembly in his high school auditorium. He is inspired to make this gesture by his father, a would-be writer who doesn't take his son's interest in the Nazis seriously and encourages him to learn more about America's oppression and exploitation of Puerto Rico.

Abraham Rodriguez

All but one of the six other stories in *The Boy Without a Flag* explore the struggles of young Nuyoricans as they enter an adult world dominated by sex, drugs, and crime with little or no understanding of the social and economic forces limiting their options. The story "Babies," for example, is the first-person narration of a pregnant teenager who is a heroin addict. She has an abortion because she realizes that El Bronx is no place for a single mom to raise a child. Nor is it a good place for Elba, the main character in two of the stories in Rodriguez's collection. In the first story, "The Lotto," Elba finds out she is pregnant but can't bring herself to have an abortion. In the sequel, "Elba," the teenage mother abandons her screaming infant for the more appealing action taking place on the streets below her apartment.

Rodriguez's depiction of the immature young men who populate El Bronx is just as hard hitting. When the narrator of "Babies" asks her boyfriend, Smiley, how he would feel about their having a baby, he warns her, "You better not get ... pregnant ... I ain't supportin no ... baby." When Elba accuses her husband Danny of abandoning her and their baby to drink beer and "smoke reefar" with his friends, he tells her it's her job to "stay home and bring up the baby."

That the fate of these characters is determined while they are still children is underscored in "Birthday Boy." Thirteen-year-old Angel is living on the streets because his mother has moved out of his family's apartment and his father beats him. When the boy is caught stealing by the police, he turns for help to the teenage drug dealer Spider, the only person he knows who can both post his bail and provide him with the kind of income he needs to get an apartment of his own.

Spider shows up again in Rodriguez's first novel, *Spidertown: A Novel*. Only now he is running an enterprise that follows a corporate business model. As a member of Spider's drug posse, sixteen-year-old Miguel drives a fancy car, sleeps with his choice of women from his mentor's stable, and no longer has to endure the violent abuses of his father. But he's not comfortable with the danger that comes with his job or the degree of obedience that Spider requires of him.

An avid reader who once thought of being a writer, Miguel dreams of hooking up permanently with Cristalena, a Latina high school student who has a dream of her own: a career. A diploma in fashion design would also allow her to break free from the rigid codes of behavior imposed on her by her parents and the restrictive roles of identity assigned to her by the male-dominated culture of El Bronx. Another important character with a dream of her own is Amelia, who becomes Miguel's close friend. Though she has dropped out of college and is into drugs, by the end of the story she decides to go back to school.

The small hope for a better life that Rodriguez offers through his portraits of Miguel, Cristalena, and their friend Amelia in *Spidertown* is reversed in *The Buddha Book: A Novel*. Also set in the South Bronx, the three central characters of Rodriguez's second novel walk away from the drug economy that has wreaked havoc on their lives, but instead of moving on to a life lived happily ever after, they head for their local police precinct.

Tired of writing narratives that followed a linear pattern and eager to explore alternative ways of telling stories, Rodriguez placed his bleak view of ghetto life within the larger context of international intrigue in *South by South Bronx*. The result is a crime story that, told from different points of view, examines the impact of terrorism and the world drug economy on the disenfranchised and despairing people who populate all his fictions.

In spite of his literary success, Abraham Rodriguez has resisted the efforts of publicity agents and journalists to turn him into a poster boy for the South Bronx. He explains his position in *Puerto Rican Voices in English: Interviews with Writers*:

> I've had some bad experiences because being the good boy who came out of the South Bronx, all they wanted to do was exploit the South Bronx to sell books, and I refused to do that. . . . I turned them down because I told them there are certain things I don't want to do . . . . Somebody told me they thought *Spidertown* was a Puerto Rican fairy tale that kids read to see that they can get out. I like that, but I hated the idea that I was being typecast into this role of social uplifter.

Nevertheless, Rodriguez has shown by his own achievements and the financial rewards he has reaped—he received a $50,000 advance for *Spidertown* and sold the novel's screen rights to Columbia Pictures for more than $300,000 — that self-empowerment is possible outside the illegal drug economy of the South Bronx. Furthermore, not all who live there are fated to become like the immature and irresponsible misfits who leap from the pages of his stories.

HOW THE SOUTH BRONX BECAME EL BRONX

I'm Puerto Rican. I am also American. I'm both. It's really stupid for anybody to say that they're completely Puerto Rican. There isn't a Puerto Rican alive that hasn't been affected by American culture, that hasn't had America inflicted upon him. I kept... trying to understand what it is to be Puerto Rican and what it means to be Puerto Rican in these times and what kind of a context can I be Puerto Rican in, in a society like this.
—Abraham Rodriguez

Early Colonialism

In December 1998 Puerto Rico accepted a gift from Russia that no one else in the United States wanted: a thirty-story, 660-ton, bronze head of Christopher Columbus. Why weren't there any other takers? In the previous twenty years, the image of Columbus as a heroic adventurer honored with a holiday on the American calendar had been revised. He was now seen as the first in a wave of Europeans

Abraham Rodriguez

Many protested the gift of a 660-ton statue of Christopher Columbus to Puerto Rico. Mayor Victor Andino of Catano examined the head of the statue when it landed on the shores of his seaside city in January 1999.

who conquered, enslaved, oppressed, and mass murdered the indigenous population of the Americas for hundreds of years. How then, Abraham Rodriguez asks, could "Puerto Ricans on the island distinguish themselves by making their own separate armistice with history?" And why should Rodriguez care about events taking place on an island he doesn't particularly like and has visited only twice? What does Puerto Rico have to do with the South Bronx?

More than you might at first think. In school, Rodriguez had been taught that he should be proud to be Puerto Rican, though no one could tell him why—and history indicated the opposite. He saw Puerto Ricans as little more than second-class citizens in a third-world community

How the South Bronx Became El Bronx

dominated by first-world people. They could die for the United States in its armed forces, but they couldn't vote for its president. Nor could its representative in Congress vote on issues that affected the Puerto Rican people. Puerto Rico couldn't determine its own foreign policy, and it couldn't allow foreign countries to compete on the island with products manufactured on the mainland.

American businesses protected by American laws set the low prices they paid for Puerto Rican raw materials as well as the high prices Puerto Ricans paid for goods manufactured in the United States. The island wasn't a nation—as Rodriguez believed until he was twelve, though he couldn't find a picture of the Puerto Rican flag in his family's almanac. It wasn't even a state, only a commonwealth—a colony of poverty and powerlessness, much like the South Bronx, only without so much violent crime. Many of the kids Rodriguez grew up with spoke little Spanish, had no use for school, ran with drug posses, carried guns, and when they did think about Puerto Rico, didn't think much of it. What was there to be proud of? To answer this question and understand the urgent fury that fuels much of Rodriguez's fiction, we need to know something about the historical relationship between Puerto Rico and the United States.

For four hundred years after Columbus's landing, Puerto Rico was a Spanish colony. But by 1897 its people enjoyed a certain amount of self-government. The island was not independent, however, and independence was what many of the Puerto Rican people wanted. Under the pretense of liberating the island from its colonial oppressor, the United States won Puerto Rico in the Spanish-American War of

1898 and quickly turned it into a colony of its own. Almost overnight the Puerto Rican people lost their limited form of self-government, and soon afterward, their economic base was dismantled as well.

Before the American takeover, Puerto Ricans subsisted on what they could produce for themselves, and on four major exports: tobacco, cattle, coffee, and sugar. After the takeover, business interests in the United States quickly created an economic infrastructure that supported the one export from which the most money could be made: sugar. Unfortunately, sugarcane is an annual crop. It takes a longer time to grow than some other crops. When it's not being either planted or harvested, there's not much for people to do. And because there wasn't much land left for them to do little on anyway, and what there was had either eroded or been turned into large, corporate-owned plantations and American military bases, a lot of Puerto Ricans found themselves out of work.

In the early decades of the twentieth century, unemployment rose by as much as 40 percent. The poverty rate wasn't far behind. Almost 80 percent of the Puerto Rican people were receiving federal aid by 1936. When the threat of German submarines patrolling the Caribbean during World War II put a halt to shipping between Puerto Rico and the mainland, some of the island's people came close to starving.

The Puerto Rican Diaspora

With the war's end in 1945, the United States became the most powerful country in the world, and Puerto Rico, with its flat fields and high unemployment rate, was seen as a perfect place to expand the nation's industrial might. Factories now grew where there once was sugarcane. Absentee business owners living on the mainland made a lot of money, but little of it wound up in the hands of the Puerto Rican people. They found work in the factories, of course, but because goods from the United States could only reach them by ship or plane, they had to pay 25 percent more than people on the

For many years, Puerto Rico's economy was dependent on one crop: sugarcane.

mainland. And because there were so many more workers on the island than jobs, their absentee employers were able to keep wages down. Puerto Ricans earned only one-third to one-half of what mainlanders earned doing similar work.

Something had to give, and it did. During the 1950s New York manufacturers needed workers in the garment industry and began recruiting heavily among Puerto Ricans living on the island. Anticipating an increase in the number of people who would fly between San Juan and New York, airlines lowered their fares. Puerto Ricans could now afford to take advantage of an opportunity to improve their standard of living. It all sounded too good to be true.

It was. Many of the Italian and Jewish descendants of earlier immigrants who previously held the jobs the immigrant Puerto Ricans would apply for had left them after discovering that the factory owners were planning to move their operations to cheaper locations outside of the city. What work was available would last only until the companies closed their doors.

That wasn't all. The only New York employers willing to pay attractive salaries outside of the garment industry wanted workers with skills that most Puerto Ricans didn't possess because the only work they knew was farm labor. When these skilled workers arrived in the city from different parts of the mainland, they needed housing. Local landlords rushed to evict their tenants and renovate their properties so they could charge higher rents and make greater profits for themselves. Because most of the Puerto Rican immigrants couldn't compete for the newly created jobs, the only housing they could afford on their low wages

How the South Bronx Became El Bronx

was in run-down buildings of the city that no landlord cared to renovate because nobody with a good job making decent money would want to live there. The landlords didn't even live there. These areas soon turned into ghettos, or barrios, of concentrated poverty.

Nevertheless, huge waves of Puerto Ricans came and settled in New York. Even though most of the available jobs would last only until the factories shut down, many migrants believed they could find new jobs before that point. These new jobs would also enable them to move out of the barrios that were forming in Brooklyn, Spanish Harlem, and the South Bronx. As they saw it, temporary jobs were better than no jobs, and every job was an opportunity to start a new life with hope for a better future.

Unfortunately, most of the temporary jobs available in the shrinking garment industry were open only to people who could do needlework. Puerto Rican women didn't traditionally work outside of their homes. It was the men who were expected to provide for the family. And they didn't do it by sewing. Because their skills limited them to menial labor, they were worse off than they had been in Puerto Rico. And worse off than the women. It was humiliating. Not only couldn't they find jobs, their wives now had to work to support their families. As more women found work outside the home, more marriages ended in divorce, more women became single parents, and once the factory jobs started leaving the city, more families entered the welfare rolls.

Nor was there much hope for the children of these families. As more Spanish-speaking students entered the public school system in Brooklyn, Spanish Harlem, and the South

Because conditions inside the tenements in which poor Puerto Rican migrants lived in the 1950s were so awful, many residents spent much of their time outside, talking to neighbors on the stoops.

How the South Bronx Became El Bronx

Bronx, many veteran teachers began requesting job assignments in other neighborhoods. It was common for schools to have one honors class for the few best and brightest and offer none of the courses that would enable any of the other students to compete for entrance into a college. Sixth-grade Puerto Rican students lagged one year behind the average black child and three years behind the average white one, and that gap increased in the later grades.

The longer many Puerto Rican students stayed in school, the less they seemed to learn, and the less they learned, the more discouraged they became. As a result, more than half of them, including Abraham Rodriguez, dropped out before they finished high school, thus swelling the ranks of the unemployed and perpetuating the role of Puerto Ricans as a source for cheap labor. With all of these human resources but little money to show for it, stores in the Puerto Rican barrios started closing down. People were forced to do without or travel outside their neighborhoods for goods and services. That meant additional money was needed for buses and subways. More and more families found themselves forced to compete economically for dilapidated apartments where they were socially isolated from all but other undereducated and unskilled Puerto Rican welfare recipients.

And where they were, they couldn't stay for long. As more and more immigrants arrived from Puerto Rico and as landlords emptied their buildings so they could be renovated to accommodate the skilled workers who would pay higher rents, the neighborhoods of Spanish Harlem became increasingly overcrowded. With the accompanying rise in gang violence and poverty, many Puerto Ricans were forced to find housing elsewhere. Some neighborhoods lost more than 70 percent of their populations, and one nine-block area lost 84 percent. Where did they go?

Most wound up in either Brooklyn or the South Bronx, and half of these weren't there for more than five years when "The Big Burn" hit. Between 1970 and 1980, more than 50 percent of all the apartments housing Puerto Ricans in Brooklyn and the Bronx were destroyed by fires deliberately set by absentee slumlords to collect insurance money and rebuild with an eye toward attracting more affluent tenants. Conditions became so unstable that some tenants even set their own apartments on fire in the hope of being placed in public housing. Buildings destroyed by arson in Brooklyn and the South Bronx between 1970 and 1980 amounted to more than 80 percent of the housing lost during the same decade for the entire United States.

Adding to the worsening situation, the city of New York completed the Bruckner Expressway in 1973. It runs right through the center of the South Bronx. That knocked off a few more buildings, leaving some blocks with only two units standing. And many of the people who had escaped the flight of neighborhood businesses, the buildings destroyed by fire, the exodus of people, and the intrusion of the highway, now periodically found themselves without water, heat, electricity, garbage services, and housing maintenance. Not only did taxicab drivers refuse to take passengers to the South Bronx, the *New York Times* wouldn't even deliver the paper there. Those still left in what many believed to be a neighborhood intentionally neglected by its city fell into a collective state of psychic despair. Something had to be done.

How the South Bronx Became El Bronx

Vandalized cars and burned-out graffitied buildings were common sights in the South Bronx of the 1970s.

During the 1980s Mayor Edward Koch spent $70,000 to make a purely cosmetic improvement. The broken windows of abandoned buildings facing the Bruckner Expressway were replaced with metal sheets featuring vinyl decals of potted flowers, opened shutters, and venetian blinds. Talk about a cover-up! It's no coincidence that one of these metal "windows" shows up on the apartment wall of the arsonist Firebug in *Spidertown*. Puerto Ricans found themselves having to work more to earn less and pay more to live on less in a neighborhood that was being likened to the bombed-out cities of

Europe during World War II. And if any complained, they knew they faced the possibility of being replaced by illegal aliens who could be kept in line with threats of deportation. Is it any wonder that some Puerto Ricans turned to drugs and crime as ways of escaping poverty and fighting oppression?

The Cruel New World

It is clear from his works that, living and writing in the South Bronx, Abraham Rodriguez had asked himself three important questions: Who am I? How did I become the person I am? To what culture—American or Puerto Rican—do I belong? In asking the first question, Rodriguez discovered the historical roots of Puerto Ricans outlined above. In asking the second, he recognized the tension that exists between his Puerto Rican roots and the dominant white culture in the United States. In asking the third, he examined how much of who he is has been determined by the social constructs of both the Puerto Rican and the dominant cultures.

Because these questions by their nature are personal, Rodriguez's writing often seems to be informed by his personal experiences. He may not have lived all the events he describes, but he seems to have seen and spoken at length with those who have. His fiction is also political and ideological. It is highly critical of those responsible for thwarting the lives of millions of Puerto Ricans who pursued the American Dream, only to remain mired in poverty and degradation.

Nor does Rodriguez hold back any punches for the kind of Puerto Ricans who are indignant when Kramer stomps on the island's flag in an episode of the *Seinfeld* television

How the South Bronx Became El Bronx

show but can't get off their couches to participate more fully in the Puerto Rican struggle for economic and social justice. Rodriguez's fiction, furthermore, is disturbing. He makes you feel his pain, frustration, and anger. At the same time, his works educate because they contain messages sent to us through plot and character about the damage being inflicted on ordinary human beings by those who sit at the social, economic, and political controls of the dominant white culture.

Rodriguez has claimed that talking about whether Puerto Ricans are losing their culture is a waste of time. They've already lost it. Whether they say they are Puerto Rican, though they may not have lived on the island, or claim to be American, though they may have been born in Puerto Rico, is irrelevant. The central issue for Puerto Rican writers, artists, and musicians today, according to Rodriguez, is how to respond to the culture that has been imposed upon them by their oppressive colonizers.

What can they do to liberate Puerto Ricans from more than a hundred years of American disrespect, exploitation, and abuse? To what extent can they create a new definition of what it means to be "Puerto Rican"? How can they achieve for Puerto Ricans everywhere a place in American history not just as victims but as contributors? Rodriguez's answer to all these questions seems to be through imaginative forms of self-expression. Writing in the Nuyorican dialect about the cruel world of El Bronx, he provides an authentic voice for the poor and disenfranchised who cannot speak for themselves about the specific experiences shared by many Puerto Ricans living in urban communities caught in the grip of a drug economy.

"Nervy, anguished, and brilliant writing by a New York Puerto Rican."—*VLS*

The Boy Without a Flag

TALES OF THE SOUTH BRONX

Abraham Rodriguez Jr.

author of *Spidertown*

The stories in *The Boy Without a Flag* are clearly drawn from the early life of Abraham Rodriguez, but they are far from being a memoir.

3
"THE BOY WITHOUT A FLAG" AND OTHER STORIES

These are the kids no one likes to talk about. I want to show them as they are, not as society wishes them to be.
—Abraham Rodriguez

ABRAHAM RODRIGUEZ BEGINS HIS collection of seven short stories with an epigraph from *The Big Money* (1963), a novel by the socially progressive American author John dos Passos: "The language of the beaten nation is not forgotten in our ears tonight." The "beaten nation," for Rodriguez's purposes, is Puerto Rico.

With the exception of the first story in *The Boy Without a Flag*, Rodriguez doesn't make an explicit connection between the dos Passos quotation and his stories. But it's clear that he sees the everyday existence of the young people in El Bronx as a part of America's continuing history of oppressing and exploiting the Puerto Rican people.

"The Boy Without a Flag"

The first story in the collection, "The Boy Without a Flag," is Rodriguez's most autobiographical story. Much of what happens to the main character also happened to him. And like the father in the story, Rodriguez's father was a would-be writer who didn't commit himself to a career in writing because he didn't think it was practical. He also believed that Puerto Rico should be independent of the United States and honored in his poetry and in conversations with his son the *Puertorriqueños* who resisted the American imperialist agenda.

Influenced by his father's nationalist rhetoric and wanting to impress him with a rebellious act of his own, as a boy, Rodriguez refused to salute the American flag during a school assembly. His teachers—all assimilated, well-meaning Puerto Ricans—responded in much the same way as those in the story. Not one could convince him to respect the country that had colonized the land of his forefathers.

Even though "The Boy Without a Flag" closely parallels the life of its author, the narrator should not be mistaken for Rodriguez. Fiction is not memoir. The narrator's experiences as well as those of other characters may have occurred in real life, but the time and place and various details may have been altered for the story. Other story elements may, of course, be solely products of the author's imagination. Rodriguez's real immigrant father, for example, held the respectable, decent-paying job of a dietitian in a hospital, but the father in "The Boy Without a Flag" performs the low-paying menial work of a counterman in Nedick's, a fast-food restaurant known for its hot dogs and orange drink.

This mural depicts a Puerto Rican flag on the crown of the Statue of Liberty; a metaphoric rendering of the sense of what it's like to be a Puerto Rican immigrant in New York City.

By turning his story into a fiction based on his life, Rodriguez frees himself from the limitation of facts so he can illustrate his conviction that American imperialism dominates the existence of Puerto Ricans living within the borders of the United States. In this way, the image of a counterman makes for a more effective victim of colonialism than that of a respectable hospital dietitian. Although many of Puerto Rico's scientists, professors, artists, and writers were attracted to the United States by academic appointments and well-paying jobs, the great majority of the immigrants to arrive on these shores were uneducated and unskilled.

"The Boy Without a Flag" opens with the precocious narrator and his friend Edwin observing Mr. Rios and Miss Colon before an assembly in their school's auditorium. The two teachers are having an affair but aren't being discreet, and the adolescents have made them objects of ridicule in an underground comic book they produce and distribute throughout the school.

When the assistant principal, Miss Marti, orders the students at an assembly to stand as the American flag is carried down the center aisle of the auditorium, the narrator hears his father's words repeating in his mind: "All this country does is abuse Hispanic nations." Because earning high grades, reading widely, and even writing book-length works of his own have not impressed his father, Rodriguez decides to win the nationalist-minded man's approval by refusing to stand up and salute the flag.

Miss Colon thinks the boy must be ill, but when he refuses to obey Mr. Rios's orders to stand at attention, he is marched to the principal's office and placed in a corner with his face to the wall. After almost two hours of standing there alone, he hears Miss Marti's approach, her "heels clacking like gunshots." She proceeds to reduce the boy to tears, telling him he's nothing more than "a snotty-nosed little kid with a lot of stupid ideas."

Because he may be afraid of exposing himself to a similar reaction at home, Rodriguez doesn't tell his hard-to-please father what he has done. Nevertheless, he again refuses to salute the American flag at the next school assembly. Though Mr. Rios commends the boy for his courage, he tells him he's got to learn to obey the rules.

That night, the youngster compares himself to one of his father's heroes, the Puerto Rican revolutionary Pedro Albizu Campos, and imagines his father preaching independence before a crowd of enthusiastic nationalists. When he discovers the next day that he can use Campos's description of Puerto Rico as an American colony to frustrate the attempts of Miss Colon and Mr. Rios to convince him to respect the flag of the United States, Rodriguez feels himself morphing from a boy who used to play with toy soldiers into a real soldier in the war against American imperialism. Once again, he finds himself in the principal's office for continuing to refuse to salute the national flag.

When the principal, Mr. Sepulveda, fails to convince the boy that he needs to follow rules and regulations, he plays the parent card: he has summoned Mr. Rodriguez to the school. Thrown off guard by this announcement, the boy expects his father to defend him and is crushed when he hears an apologetic Mr. Rodriguez agree with the principal:

Abraham Rodriguez

The Puerto Rican revolutionary and Nationalist Party leader Pedro Albizu Campos was a hero to the narrator of the story "The Boy Without a Flag."

"You have to obey the rules. You can't do this. It's wrong." Mr. Rodriguez may be trying to protect his son from further punishment, but the boy concludes that the enemy against whom his father spoke so convincingly in the comfort of their living room has already taken possession of him, just as it has the teachers and the principal.

"The Boy Without a Flag" and Other Stories

On its most basic level, "The Boy Without a Flag" is a story of maturation through loss of innocence. A boy refuses to salute the American flag because he wants to win his nationalist father's approval. When his father doesn't support him, the boy finds out the armchair revolutionary is not the hero he thought he was—the universal theme of the child realizing the parent isn't perfect. Disillusioned by what he calls "my father's betrayal," the boy loses some respect for his father. But he also learns to accept through his love for his father the lesson that compromise is sometimes necessary for survival. In doing so, the boy matures beyond the scope of his adolescent classmates.

"The Boy Without a Flag" is also a fine example of literature as social commentary. Its title is an allusion to "Man Without a Country," a short story written in 1863 by Edward Everett Hale about a man who condemns the United States and is prohibited from ever again setting foot on its shores. But the title also reflects the anger of Puerto Ricans living in a country where they often feel exploited, disrespected, and oppressed. This treatment is symbolized in the respective positions of the American and Puerto Rican flags as they are carried into the school auditorium. The American flag is described as a "great star-spangled unfurling," while the "smaller, subordinate, less confident" Puerto Rican flag clings to its pole. When the character Rodriguez tries to rebel, he, like many Puerto Ricans who yearn for an independent nation, is beaten back by the guardians of the dominant culture, in this instance the school's teachers and administrators.

The triumph of the school authorities may also be seen as Rodriguez's comment on the relatively easy dismissal and consequent ineffectiveness of the Latino culture's historic revolutionaries. He has given their names not to the rebellious teenagers but to the weak-minded supporters of the status quo. Juan Ginés de Sepúlveda, a sixteenth-century theologian who argued that Native Americans were not fully human, turns up as the school principal who tells the character Rodriguez that his rebellious behavior is not going to look good on his record. Filiberto Ojeda Ríos, founder of the Los Macheteros revolutionary group in 1976, is now the foolish rodent-like teacher Mr. Rios, who tells Rodriguez, "You're just a puny kid." José Martí, who died in the nineteenth-century Cuban rebellion against Spain, has become Miss Marti, the insensitive assistant principal who has "reptile legs" and the "mouth of a lizard." "You're nothing," she tells the boy. "You're not worth a damn."

Miss Colon, albeit much less aggressively and in the pink stockings that reflect the kind of feather-brained thinking that inspires her to make out in the janitor's closet with Mr. Rios and invite her glue-sniffing husband to address the class, continues the colonization of the mind initiated in 1492 by Cristóbal Colón (Christopher Columbus). When she and Mr. Rios tell the boy he should salute the flag, and he challenges them by saying, "I thought I was free," Miss Colon responds feebly: "You are. That's why you should salute the flag." No one in the story bears the name of Pedro Albizu Campos, but the character Rodriguez likens himself to the Puerto Rican revolutionary, a comparison that comes up short when the boy is defeated so quickly by the school principal while Campos languished until his death in a United States prison.

"The Boy Without a Flag" and Other Stories

Finally, "The Boy Without a Flag" is the story of a young Nuyorican who is trying to develop a sense of history and self-worth but is caught between two competing worlds: that of his nationalistic father, who has no respect for any "Yankee flag-waver," and that of his school's rigidly pro-American educators. Both believe they have the boy's best interest at heart. Ashamed and defeated, the narrator accepts with pain the human imperfection of his father and, because he is powerless, agrees to obey the educators' rules, but he also accepts the challenge to search alone for a peace beyond "the bondage of obedience."

"No More War Games"

"No More War Games" tells the story of nearly twelve-year-old Nilsa, who loves to fight with and defeat boys in the abandoned buildings and empty lots of her neighborhood. Her good friend Cha-Cha, however, has recently given up on "kid stuff" and moved on to purple eye shadow, cherry-flavored lip gloss, and dark red nails. "It's the only way to get guys," she explains.

Walking past an abandoned building, Nilsa and another friend, nine-year-old Maria, are ambushed by two boys who throw rocks and bottles at them from a third-story window. Maria flees, but Nilsa rushes into the building feeling like a hero in a war movie "only this was better because she was a girl, a lioness, or cheetah-ess, or whatever." She surprises the boys and captures one of them. Commanding her prisoner to kiss her on the lips, Nilsa imagines herself as the kind of woman who is both powerful enough to make boys

Between 1970 and 1975 it is estimated that there were more than 68,000 fires in the South Bronx, or more than thirty-three every night for five years.

fear her and sexy enough to be attractive to them. But the boy won't cooperate, so Nilsa asks him whether it's because she's not "pretty enough." When he tells Nilsa she's only "all right," the girl's face stings with disappointment and embarrassment. Cha-Cha was right. If Nilsa wants to have a boyfriend, she's going to have to style her hair, pick out the right color lipstick, and start wearing "tight French jeans."

Like "The Boy Without a Flag," "No More War Games" is a coming-of-age story in which the protagonist faces a

"The Boy Without a Flag" and Other Stories

choice between rebellion and submission in the proverbial battle of the sexes. In the same way that the Rodriguez character rebelled against his teachers' patriotic views but submitted to the "bondage of obedience" when his father failed to support him, so too does Nilsa resist the sexual stereotype her friend Cha-Cha encourages her to adopt until she realizes she must conform to male expectations if she wants to "get" a boyfriend.

For both the boy in "The Boy Without a Flag" and Nilsa in "No More War Games," crossing the threshold of adulthood is not just an increased level of awareness; it is also an acceptance of loss. The boy accepts the fact that his father is not a hero, and Nilsa realizes that if she wants to get a boyfriend she has to stop beating boys at their own games. Each also must give up something of who they are—the boy his rebellion and the girl her tomboy ways—if they want to succeed in an adult world where following convention is more important than being true to yourself.

But is their gain worth their sacrifice? The Rodriguez boy in "The Boy Without a Flag" has good reasons not to salute a flag he sees as a symbol of imperialism. He also has the constitutional right to say what he thinks. And given the history of American and Puerto Rican relations, many would consider his behavior appropriate. In another school with different teachers, perhaps the boy's rebellion would be seen as an opportunity to discuss the ways Puerto Ricans have been exploited by American business interests and what might be done to right the wrongs that have been covered up by history. But in this boy's school, where all the educators are assimilated Puerto Ricans, he learns "how important obedience is" even when that obedience includes forced displays of patriotism at school assemblies.

And what about Nilsa in "No More War Games"? Though she feels Cha-Cha looks like a clown when she wears makeup, Nilsa discovers she has to stop engaging in war games and start appearing in ways that are conventionally attractive to men if she wants their attention. She may not fully understand why the aggression that some consider sexy in a man isn't also considered sexy in a woman, but she's learning. Under the tutelage of her friend Cha-Cha, it won't be long before she starts looking as though she just stepped out of a cosmetics advertisement. Nor will it be long before the boys she wants to attract begin looking at her as a sex object at their disposal.

"Babies"

The unnamed narrator in "Babies" is a sixteen-year-old heroin addict who wants to have a baby. Neglected and unloved as a child, she lives in a run-down tenement with Smiley, a high school dropout who smokes pot "like a stove" and supplies her with heroin. The narrator admires him because she believes that his stabbing his father for banging his mother around "like a Ping-Pong ball" was heroic. Smiley, however, does not want to father a child. He claims that its all he can do to supply the narrator with the expensive heroin he exchanges for sex and uses to feed her addiction, keep her dependent on him, and control her behavior.

Sara and Diana provide additional reasons why Rodriguez's narrator should think twice about having a baby.

"The Boy Without a Flag" and Other Stories

When the narrator goes to visit her, Sara can't remember where she has left her two-week-old infant and doesn't want to talk about where the baby might be. "It's around," she tells the Narrator. "Around" turns out be either with Madgie "outside the bakery" or "by the liquor store." When the narrator tells Sara, "You gotta be responsible an take care of your baby," the negligent mother turns defensive: "Tell me I don't care bout my kid. I bet if you had a kid, you do better?" In the end, the narrator learns from Sara the fate of her baby: "It's gone."

When we meet Diana, she is trying to avoid her mother, who is determined to keep her daughter from ending up on the streets by convincing her to abort her seven-month-old fetus. The mother finally catches up to Diana and beats her so badly that the teenager has to be taken by ambulance to a hospital, where she loses her baby. When the narrator runs into Diane sometime later, the fetus is now a history that's on its way to being forgotten through drugs.

The narrator's maternal instincts are in the right place—she tells Sara she should take better care of her baby, and she tries to prevent Diana's mother from beating up her pregnant daughter—but the place where she lives isn't right for a baby. Especially with men like the father of Sara's child, who "ain't got time for no babies," and the father of Diana's, who hasn't been seen for six months.

When the narrator asks Smiley what he thinks about having a child, the man angrily replies that if she ever gets pregnant, he's out the door. Each man's response reflects a view commonly held by the subset of Puerto Rican men that Rodriguez writes about, namely, that women are solely

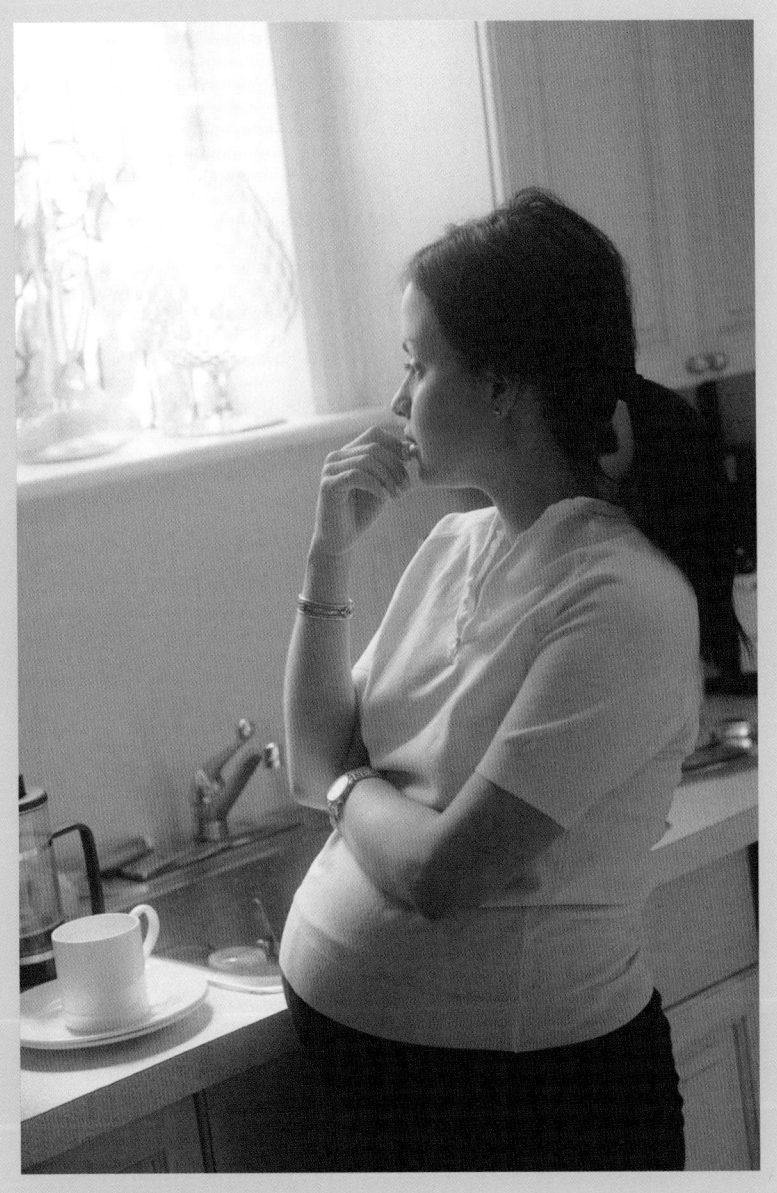

For many girls in the ghetto, having a baby was a way to have something that they felt was their own in a world in which they had absolutely nothing.

responsible for any babies they might have. When Rodriguez's narrator eventually becomes pregnant, she assesses the future awaiting her and her unborn child and decides to have an abortion: "Smiley din't know thea was a tiny baby inside of me, but I knew it. I also knew thea was a part of me in that baby, an a part of him, an zero plus zero equals zero."

Like the Rodriguez character in "The Boy Without a Flag" and Nilsa in "No More War Games," the narrator of "Babies" sacrifices an important part of her identity to the powerful forces that have been arrayed against her. What's different is that she doesn't have much choice. She wants to have a baby, but to try to raise a child as a heroin-addicted, single parent in the impoverished, violent, drug-ridden environment Rodriguez depicts doesn't make much sense. Especially when, like her friends Sara and Diana, she is only a baby herself.

"The Lotto" and "Elba"

"The Lotto" and its sequel "Elba" expand Rodriguez's view of El Bronx as a breeding ground for immature mothers and irresponsible fathers. In the first story, a junior high school student, Dalia, awakens frightened after dreaming of babies being pulled like rabbits out of magic hats. It's no wonder. Five days earlier, she had told her boyfriend Ricky that she might be pregnant. His response? "You blew it big time." Ricky hasn't been seen since.

Dalia confides in her friend Elba, who buys her a home pregnancy test. Dalia is greatly relieved when the test reveals that she is not pregnant, but Elba is not so lucky. Nor can she bring herself to have an abortion. "I don't like school anyway," she tells Dalia as she resigns herself to a life of welfare checks, run-down apartments, soaring crime rates, debilitating drugs, and unshared responsibilities.

Running parallel to the story of the two girls is that of Dalia's mom, Rosa, who pins her hopes for a better future on the New York State lottery. She believes that God sends her—through dreams—the numbers she needs to win the $50 million jackpot. If only she could interpret the messages accurately! If only the numbers didn't have so many different combinations! If only the charms in her lucky magic box would work! If only her husband would stop offending God with his foul language. If he only he had faith! If only. As Rosa and her husband watch the disappointing results of yet another lottery drawing on television, Dalia secretly conducts a winning lottery of a different nature in the bathroom: she isn't pregnant. Of course Rosa misinterprets her daughter's tears of joy as tears of loss over the lottery drawing and tries to comfort her by hugging her and telling her that "God still cares."

We've seen these themes played out in other Rodriguez stories: teenagers who live in El Bronx have little control over their own lives; the future of any babies they might have is not promising; and immature, irresponsible men like Ricky think only of themselves. What's new in "The Lotto" is Rodriguez's representation of religion as superstitious, powerless, and irrelevant. According to him, people foolish enough to pray to God might just as well place their faith in the lottery and condemn themselves to lives of perpetual, unrewarded hopefulness.

Rodriguez's choice of title for the story confirms this

"The Boy Without a Flag" and Other Stories

view. The "lotto" is a reference to the lotus flower—called "el loto" in Spanish. In classical mythology the loto was supposed to make people lazy, which is the effect the lottery has on Dalia's mom. Praying to God to improve one's life instead of trying to find a job, Rodriguez is telling us, is as fruitless as playing the lottery.

A second theme indicated by Rodriguez's choice of title may be its reference to an old Spanish saying: *La vida es una tombola* or "Life is a lottery." From this perspective, almost everything that happens in this story—from getting pregnant to winning the lottery—can be seen as either a random accident or a stroke of luck.

In "Elba," we learn what has happened to Dalia's friend since she has had her baby. Elba wants to be a good mother, but she is having trouble coping with the demands of motherhood without the help of her husband Danny. The story opens on the ominous note of a wailing siren, as Elba lies in bed while her baby cries to her from the living room: "The baby's screech was a tiny air-raid siren wailing inside her skull, pulling, drawing blood from her."

Another reference to classical mythology? Sirens were sea nymphs whose call no one could resist. They used their voices to lure sailors in passing ships to their destruction among the cliffs that lined the shore. We name the sirens that screech from our ambulances, fire trucks, and police cars after these half-human, half-bird creatures; only today the call is a response to danger—just like the baby's cries.

A second warning of what's to come is the baby's resemblance to his father, Danny. When Elba insists that he stay home and help her take care of their child, he tells her, "You gotta stay home an bring up the baby. Thass it. You wanted marriage, you got it." And he's had it. He beats his wife "motionless and senseless" and heads for the door.

Traumatized by the beating and the look of "hatred and anger" that twisted Danny's face, Elba can no longer bear him or his son. After reflecting on the romance that once was and the violence that now is, a "terrible defiance" comes over her and she decides two can play the same game. She showers, slips into a provocative outfit, picks up her crying baby "as if it were Danny," and drops him into his crib from such a height that he remains in the same "motionless and staring" state that Danny left her in earlier in the story. She then leaves the volume on the stereo blaring and heads out the door of their roach-ridden prison of an apartment. The breeze that rushes to greet her in the stairwell is cool and refreshing.

"Birthday Boy" and "Roaches"

Girls and their babies aren't the only ones who have it tough in El Bronx. Angel, making plans to rob an apartment, has just turned thirteen. His girlfriend is pregnant, his father beats him, and Spider is pressuring him to run drugs.

Angel, as his name suggests, is a good boy, and his relationship with his father was healthy until his mother started having an affair. When his father found out, he beat her until she fled their home. He then blamed Angel for his wife's infidelity and began pounding the boy "from one end of the house to the other."

Angel finds a less violent home on the streets of El Bronx. This is where he hooks up with Spider, who finds him places to spend the night and introduces the boy to pot, theft, assault, and sixteen-year-old Gloria. Angel resists the temptation to join Spider's drug posse, however, until Gloria becomes pregnant, he gets caught stealing, and there's only one person who can post his bail, free him from his father, set him up with an apartment of his own, and provide him with the income he needs to support a family. "I'm better than any federal program you can name," Spider tells Angel. "I got a buncha grade-schoolers pickin up crack vials on the street. I pay um a dime a vial. Beats cans! I call that my 'entry level' position."

How far Angel will fall can be estimated in the attitude and behavior of Joey, a drug-dealing lowlife in "Roaches"—one of Rodriguez's most powerfully written short stories. "Roaches" was published in 1992 in *Iguana Dreams*, an anthology of Latino literature, but its territory is the same as that of the stories in *The Boy Without a Flag*: sex, drugs, violence, oppressive gender conventions, and the ongoing struggle between inadequate parents and their immature children.

Joey is seventeen when Annette, the girlfriend whom he calls his wife, is kidnapped by a rival drug gang, but he's too busy playing in a pool competition for the sexual favors of Yolanda to be concerned. Three days later, the body of Annette shows up in a trash bag. The police assigned to the case have seen carved-up dead bodies before, but this is their first teenage girl. She's pregnant too. Or was. Officers Shaw and Sanchez are already familiar with Joey's stoic persona from their investigation into Annette's disappearance, but they can't wait to see the look on his face when he sees what's happened to his so-called wife: the recognition, the horror, the disintegration of his constantly indifferent facial expression. Joey, however, remains unmoved, his eyes looking down on Annette as if she's no more than a "squashed roach." And his only comment? "Business is business."

The police might have been able to rescue Annette if they'd had some help from the people in the neighborhood, but the girl's parents are so frightened of Joey, that they can do little more than report her missing.

Their younger daughter, who is on the same life-and-probably-death path as her sister, refuses to cooperate with the officers because she doesn't want to be a snitch. The police, after all, are the enemy of Joey, Annette, and everyone else involved in the drug trade. When possible eyewitnesses are interviewed, their response is always the same: "I no see nothen." An almost absurd but equally despairing exception is Old Man Benitez, who sees everything through the 3D glasses that provide him with a graphic, comic book intensity he claims is better than watching television. But he won't talk to the police either. "They don't got no feeling," Officer Shaw says about kids like Joey, but he could just as well be talking about adults like Benitez: "They act like they're alive, but they're not."

"Fake Moon" and "Short Stop"

A rare adult point of view is featured in "Fake Moon," which was posted in the electronic magazine *Nerve.com* in 2002, and in "Short Stop," which appears in *The Boy Without a Flag*. Ada, the forty-three-year-old wife of Raul in "Fake Moon," is trapped in a tired, sexless marriage. She

"The Boy Without a Flag" and Other Stories

compensates for her husband's lack of attention in general and for his ignoring her birthday in particular by drinking at the rear window of their apartment and watching a young male neighbor masturbate to pornographic movies. After discovering Ada's secret, Raul leads a group of irate husbands, whose neglected and frustrated wives have also been spying on the man, to beat up what they see as a threat to their masculinity.

The story ends with Ada running down the stairs of her apartment to call the police to save her neighbor. Whether or not the police arrive in time, it is clear that the women's passive attempt to escape sexually from their unhappy marriages has no more chance of a satisfactory outcome than Rosa's praying to God for financial deliverance in "The Lotto." Equally as obvious is Rodriguez's criticism of the men, who refuse to accept their share of the responsibility that led the women to fantasize about their neighbor. Instead of paying more attention to their wives, they choose to punish him.

A different sort of man appears in "Short Stop," one whose attempts to save the life of a suicidal young woman reveal a sympathetic attitude toward Nuyorican youth that is mostly absent in the characters who inhabit Rodriguez's other short fiction. Marty, a subway motorman who's having a bad week, sees a girl in sneakers sitting on a maintenance catwalk as his train enters a tunnel. He stops the train, gets out, and approaches the girl, who tells him, "Please juss run me ova." Although annoyed with having to deal with this disruption to his schedule, Marty is moved by the young woman's plight and gently leads her back to his car. At the last stop, he turns her over to the transit police, and they release her after asking a few routine questions. When he sees the teenager moments later heading for a tunnel where no motorman would be able to stop a train before hitting her, Marty runs after the girl "as if he had an errand."

Marty's compassion for the suicidal young woman is underscored by the way he treats others in the story. He lights the cigarette of a homeless person even though smoking is prohibited in subway stations, risks his own life when he refuses to open the doors to his train and allow armed teenagers to harm his passengers, warns his conductor that she will lose her job if she keeps announcing the wrong stops, gets along well with his fellow worker Clint, and loves his wife Melissa.

Marty also yearns to be a father, but he and his wife have not been able to conceive a child after three years of trying. "This'll be the year we have a kid, man," he tells himself, "it's gotta be." Further evidence of Marty's desire to nurture becomes apparent when he tells the suicidal woman, "You juss a baby." Contrasting with Marty's caring behavior are the teenage boys who try to enter his train with a pulled gun, the conductor who doesn't care that she incorrectly announces each approaching subway stop, and the transit police who release the suicidal woman despite knowing she is a danger to herself and others.

Given the officers' indifferent attitude toward the suicidal woman and the inability of Marty to influence her behavior, "Short Stop" might also be entitled "Another Fake Moon." Only this time, the futility is not the ineffectual escapism through fantasy Rodriguez depicted in his earlier story but the kind of charity that yields no benefit. No matter what he does, Marty cannot stop the woman from trying to kill herself. Nevertheless, it is to his credit that he tries. Not many of the men in Rodriguez's stories would.

And what about this unnamed woman who wants to end her life? All we know about her is what she tells us: "I'm sick of fightin." Rodriguez's omission of any clue as to why the woman planned to jump in front of Marty's oncoming train led the critic Daniel Frick to conclude that the young author's "ambitions exceed his present abilities." In fact, Frick sums up the entire collection of stories in *The Boy Without a Flag* as "a failure of imagination."

While it is true that Rodriguez provides no background information on the suicidal woman, it's difficult to believe a writer of his talent lacks the imagination to create one. Nor is he short of resources for personal histories in the people he knows and events he has witnessed or learned about while living in the South Bronx. Perhaps Rodriguez omitted the background information about the suicidal woman because he felt it would take away from his readers' focus on the subway motorman. It is, after all, his story. We see the woman as he does.

More than likely, Rodriguez left out a specific explanation for why the woman wants to throw herself in front of a train because he wants his readers to think of the other teenage women who appear in his stories—Nilsa in "No More War Games," the unnamed narrator and her friends Sara and Diana in "Babies," Dalia in "The Lotto," and Elba in "Elba"—and imagine their own versions of the story that led the desperate girl in "Short Stop" to tell Marty, "I wanna die."

The failure of imagination, then, may very well be Frick's for seeing Rodriguez's stories as individual narratives and not parts of a collective whole.

"The Subway King"

"The Subway King," which appears in *Story* magazine, is not included in the collection *The Boy Without a Flag*, but it completes Rodriguez's short story collage of disaffected youth in the South Bronx. The works discussed so far include several teenage mothers, some dysfunctional parents, and a few caring adults. This story presents an up-close and personal look at the troubled teenage boys who become the fathers of the teenage mothers, baffle their elders, and have no respect for conventional authority, much less their fellow human beings.

Three of the four teenage gang members who appear in "The Subway King" strongly resemble the boys with the loaded gun who tried to get onto Marty's train in "Short Stop." While Joyboy lands flying kicks against the windows of the subway car they are traveling on, Ritchie tells Gooch to show the gun he carries to an amphetamine-pumped Willyboy. Gooch takes out the gun and holds it with the same care as "if he had just delivered a baby." Ritchie places the gun in Willyboy's hand and orders the eleven-year-old to shoot out one of the train windows. Aware of the new sense of power afforded him by the gun, Willyboy sees his buddies as "roaches" he'd like to "splatter." Fortunately for his buddies, who tear down and then tear up the advertisements that line the subway car, Willyboy settles for shattering glass.

"The Boy Without a Flag" and Other Stories

Broken glass, shredded paper, and even walls spray-painted in blood red can't compete with the thrill of a mugging, however, and the boys take advantage of an opportunity to beat and rob a student in an adjacent car. They also throw an elderly woman to the floor of the train and steal her purse. Aboveground, the exhilarated boys are unsettled by a police car that happens to cruise by, but once he feels they are safe, Ritchie starts running and laughing like a maniac. The others, with "laughter bubbling out in yelps and howls," run after him.

The New York subways were plastered with graffiti in the 1970s by disaffected youth saying "Look at me." The cry for help and attention was ignored as the subways were cleaned up.

67

Abraham Rodriguez

The specific reasons why these boys came to think, feel, and act the ways they do in "The Subway King" are as unclear as the the thoughts that might have led the suicidal young woman in "Short Stop" to want to leap in front of a subway. Rodriguez's reason for not providing this background information for the characters in "Short Stop," however, may be different than it was in "The Subway King" and may answer the question of why he doesn't include background information for most of the characters in his short stories.

With the exception of "The Boy Without a Flag" and his novels, there is no sense of history and little sense of culture in any of his fiction beyond what his characters come across on the streets of their wretched lives. In other words, Rodriguez confines his writing to the present because his characters live relentlessly and unreflectively in the present. That's the way he created them, and that's the way he wants his readers to experience them. For the characters as well as for the readers' experience of the characters' lives, there is no life beyond the borders of El Bronx and no future beyond the reality of what already is.

Conclusion

Ritchie, Gooch, Willyboy, and Joyboy of "The Subway King"—as their names suggest—are kids. Dangerous kids. And like many of the teenagers who appear in Rodriguez's stories, they are dangers to themselves as well as to others. Think, for example, of the unnamed narrator in "Babies": a sixteen-year-old heroin addict who wants to have a baby with a drug-dealing ex-con. And what about her friends

Sara and Diana? Sara can't remember where she has left her newborn and is willing to give it away to the first person willing to take it. Her boyfriend "ain't got time for no babies" either. Diana wants to keep her soon-to-be-born baby, but her mother—while shouting expressions of affection such as "my daughter" and "My Baby"—beats her into a miscarriage. Nor is Diana's boyfriend any help; he hasn't been seen in six months.

Ricky, in "The Lotto," cradles Dalia like "a little girl" in a drug dealer's crib but disappears when he learns she might be pregnant. Fortunately for Dalia, the feared pregnancy turns out to be a false alarm. Dalia's friend Elba is not so lucky: she gets pregnant but can't bring herself to have an abortion because of her love for her boyfriend Danny. In the sequel, "Elba," both motherhood and marriage end in disaster. Danny refuses to accept his roles as a father and husband, beats Elba senseless, and flees their apartment. In defiance, Elba drops and then abandons her screaming infant and heads for some street action of her own.

Angel, in "Birthday Boy," celebrates his unlucky thirteenth birthday by getting arrested. He is later lured into Spider's web of drugs and crime so he can rent an apartment and support his pregnant sixteen-year-old girlfriend Gloria. Seventeen-year-old Joey in "Roaches" has become so hardened to the violent world of El Bronx he remains unmoved when detectives Shaw and Sanchez show him the butchered remains of Annette and their unborn child. For Rodriguez, "People are "almost taught to be this way. You are almost indoctrinated. When you look around you, you will see that this place is a closed door. There is nothing out there."

Of course, as Rodriguez himself has demonstrated, there are ways out of the South Bronx. The boy Rodriguez, who reads books the size of milk crates in "The Boy Without a Flag," is not likely to wind up in Spider's web, though the author Rodriguez did spend eight months running with a drug posse led by a former school friend. One of the results of this "research," in which Rodriguez witnessed some activity he wishes he hadn't, is the more fully developed Spider in his first novel *Spidertown*.

Sanchez, the detective in "Roaches" who considers himself an example of someone who grew up in the barrio and did not become a criminal, also plays a more significant role in *Spidertown*. By the time he appears in *South by South Bronx*, however, Sanchez's integrity as a law enforcement officer has been compromised. The motorman Marty in "Short Stop" has yet to reappear in another Rodriguez story, but along with the character Rodriguez in "The Boy Without a Flag," he can be seen as someone who has not been negatively impacted by the poverty and crime that define so much of El Bronx.

These characters, however, are exceptions. For most of the teenage boys who inhabit Rodriguez's landscape, there are only two choices: drop out of school, take low-paying jobs, and live the rest of your life in poverty, or join the drug trade, make some money, and die young or behind bars. The range for girls is even more limited. Pregnancy followed by abortion or abuse is the option for almost every one of them. They're expected to dress provocatively, be sexually permissive, and then take care of any children they might have without help from the men who fathered them.

Many of Rodriguez's female characters rebel against

the oppressive roles that have been assigned them, but their rebellions rarely result in independence. Most of the time their efforts are rewarded with more pain, the kind that is so severe and unrelenting it often forces them to self-medicate through the most powerful illegal drug available: heroin. El Bronx, according to Rodriguez, "is a lousy place to live."

SPIDER TOWN

UNA NOVELA DE ABRAHAM RODRÍGUEZ

"Asombrante, sexy, exuberante... Rodríguez capta una verdad de nuestra época."
—Los Angeles Times Book Review

Spidertown was the first of Abraham Rodriguez's novels. It is a shocking entrée into the worlds of those with no power; that is the world that resonates for and from Abraham Rodriguez.

4

SPIDERTOWN: A NOVEL AND "BAPTISM UNDER FIRE"

> Some people see it (*Spidertown*) as a bleak message; some people see it as a message of hope. For me, it's my way of expressing my feelings about things.
> —Abraham Rodriguez

Spidertown: A Novel

In every culture, there is a center of power. Those at the center or close to it often determine what is valued most by the people who live in that culture. Think, for example, of most of our leaders in government and business, especially those in the advertising and entertainment industries. They are the ones who influence to a large extent the ways most people in this country look, think, and feel. They are the ones who determine through the popular culture what the rest of us hold to be important, beautiful, and true. Consequently, anyone or anything that does not conform to the viewpoints held by most people is often considered irrelevant, ugly, or false.

Most of the people at the center of power in the United States are rich, white, male, heterosexual Christians who speak and write in what is generally referred to as "standard English" —the kind you are most likely to hear over the radio or see on television news broadcasts.

With few exceptions, the less you have in common with those at the center, the further removed you are from influencing what's believed to be important in the culture. Imagine, for example, that you're a poor single mom for whom English is a second language. You might have a lot to say, but how would you get your message heard? And the more marginalized you are, the more you feel as if you don't belong. What if, in addition to being a poor single mom who doesn't speak English very well, you are a teenager who didn't graduate from high school? Now imagine that you're also a person of color. And a lesbian. You get the point: the more you differ from most of the people in the broader culture, the more you feel you're not one of "them." You feel like you're some kind of "other." You don't always know exactly what that "other" is, but you always know exactly what it's not. It's not anything that's admired, respected, or celebrated in the cultural mainstream.

The world depicted in Abraham Rodriguez's short stories and first novel is about as far from the culture's center of power as you can get and still be in the United States. Told from the viewpoint of sixteen-year-old drug runner Miguel, *Spidertown: A Novel* is a hard-hitting exposé of the extent to which poverty, crime, misogyny, and violence define so much of the South Bronx. It's also a protest novel. By telling his story from the viewpoint of history's victims, Rodriguez not only challenges the dominant culture's negative stereotypes of Puerto Ricans as poor, loud, violent, uneducated,

Spidertown: A Novel and "Baptism Under Fire"

The people portrayed in *Spidertown* are about as far from the mainsprings of power as it is possible to get.

sex-crazed, drug-dealing, criminally inclined, hip-hopping welfare cheats who wear too much makeup, boast too many gold chains, listen to too much salsa music at too high volumes, and should be spending on their too many children the money they throw away on too many tattoos done in bad taste, he also undermines the dominant culture's hierarchical order of what s important and attractive. In other words, it becomes more difficult for prejudiced readers to accept the

75

Abraham Rodriguez

views of Puerto Ricans that appear most frequently in the media once they've discovered the circumstances that lead to Miguel's running with a drug posse and the guilt and shame that motivate his redemption. And the more these readers come to know Miguel, Amelia, Cristalena, and Sanchez, the more likely they are to see Puerto Ricans as people rather than as stereotypes created and reinforced by the dominant culture. Even two of the so-called bad guys, Firebug and Spider, come off as somewhat deserving of understanding and sympathy. By challenging his readers to examine traditional stereotypes, giving voice to the oppressed people he writes about, and providing examples of characters who have escaped from and succeeded beyond the mean streets of El Bronx, Rodriguez presents an opportunity for people of all ages, races, and cultures to to create their own definitions of what's normal, right, and true.

The "lowercase people"
Miguel

One of the most effective ways to subvert the negative viewpoints of a dominant culture and introduce new, multiple, and more culturally diverse perspectives is to write an engaging novel about some of the attractive people who live in a specific marginal location. Miguel—a more fully realized combination of Angel in "The Birthday Boy" and the narrator in "The Boy Without a Flag"—is sixteen, handsome, well built, well off, and from the South Bronx. He doesn't do homework, drives a customized Chevy Impala, has his choice of women from Spider's collection of prostitutes,

Spidertown: A Novel and "Baptism Under Fire"

lives in an apartment that he shares with his friend Firebug, makes more money than most adults, and sits on a nest egg of $8,000 that he claims he has to keep hidden because he isn't old enough to have a bank account. But not having his money protected in a bank account is a small price to pay for the lucrative life of crime he leads.

Miguel also reads: Leo Tolstoy, Charles Dickens, and Mark Twain are only a few of the many classic writers on his shelf. Miguel once dreamed of being a writer but gave that up when he found out that there was no such thing as a Puerto Rican writer. He had never seen a book written by one, anyway. The closest he came to realizing his dream was in the seventh grade when he wrote an essay about his father: a once-muscular, now flabby, ex-Marine who screamed a lot and routinely beat his wife. When Miguel realized while writing the essay that he had recently made $400 from a single drug deal and the best his father could do working full-time as a construction worker was $132 a week, he gave up his ambition to write and left the classroom for life as a runner in Spider's posse.

Miguel's father eventually abandoned his family, but when he was replaced by one of the many new men in Miguel's mom's life, Miguel also moved out. The nineteen-year-old drug entrepreneur Spider found him a place to live, assumed the mantle of a surrogate father, and began grooming the fourteen-year-old to be his lieutenant.

Miguel thinks of himself as an adult. He has freedom, money, and a career. But something isn't right. His roommate Firebug's girlfriend, Amelia, tells him it's Miguel that's not right: "The problem is you got heart, baby. A real thinking loner. Out to get what he can, but filled with remorse."

Miguel doesn't want to hear he's a sensitive soul who yearns for something more meaningful than money, sex, and a fancy car even though he knows it's true. He also knows that what he's doing is wrong. When he falls in love with Cristalena, he tells her he works in a lumber company because he knows how she feels about drug dealers: they make her wish she had a machine gun. When Miguel argues that drug running is just a business like any other, Cristalena replies, "Business nothing. This block used to be nice once, little kids playing, old men playing dominoes. You could hang out. Not now, not anymore. These creeps have stolen it, killed it."

What's a poor sixteen-year-old drug runner to do? Get out of the drug business, go back to school, get an education, find a job, marry Cristalena, and write a best-selling novel about a sixteen-year-old drug runner, of course. But how? Without Spider, there is no car, no apartment, no source of income, and no more living the American Dream. Those things brought him some happiness and a lot of freedom. What would his return to conventional living have to offer? Homework, curfews, and once his crime subsidy ran out, shoveling fries at McDonald's. How do you give up the American Dream without sinking into the American Nightmare?

If only the choices were that simple. If only the drug business really was a business you could walk away from like any other. If only it didn't come with its own set of rules and regulations. And punishments. When Miguel's showing up late for a drug drop risks the life of a client, Spider feels betrayed. To what extent can his protégé now be trusted? To test him, Spider has Miguel deliver a payoff of $10,000 to the corrupt police who patrol the hood, but he also gives orders to have the tires on the boy's car slashed in case he has some ideas about taking off with the money. Miguel passes the loyalty test but Spider, believing the boy would also benefit from a lesson in responsibility, allows him to be severely beaten by the client whose life he endangered. Now it's Miguel's turn to feel betrayed: "I quit, man. I'm through spiderman, you let me down. I can't trust 'ju no more. There's jus' no way."

That's what he thinks. Miguel can't work for anybody else even if he wanted to. Spider won't let him. When the collapse of his status as lieutenant-in-training, the withdrawal of male bonding by Spider, and a multitude of bruises administered by one of Spider's clients and his posse aren't enough to persuade Miguel that there is no life for him outside of the drug industry, he winds up with two bullets in his back.

Recuperating in a hospital under the watchful gazes of his mom, Amelia, and Cristalena, Miguel meets a new kind of father figure: Detective Sanchez. Sanchez, who made his first appearance in "Roaches" and plays a major role as a compromised detective in Rodriguez's latest novel, *South by South Bronx*, wants to bring Spider to justice, but he's also interested in Miguel's well-being. His paternal behavior quickly restores the boy's confidence in adult males and provides the intimacy he wants from them. The two also speak the important language of books. When Miguel hands over to Sanchez the cassette on which Spider has recorded his life of crime, he not only ensures Spider's incarceration and

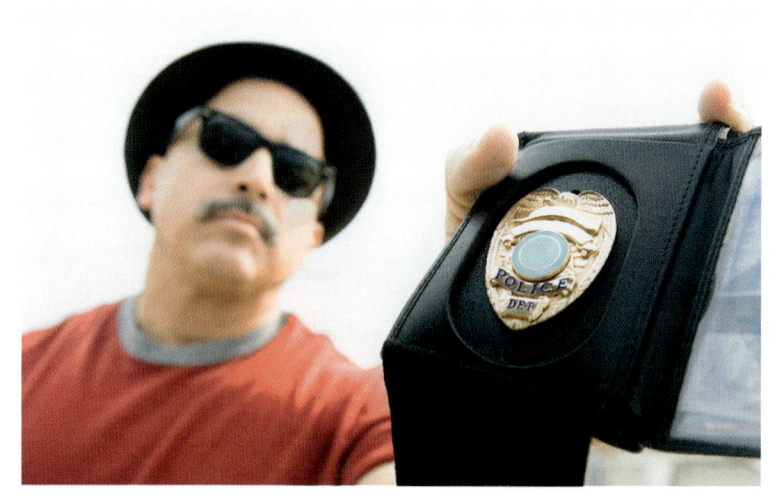

Bad cops and a good detective have strong roles to play in *Spidertown*.

protects himself from any retaliation by his former mentor, he also frees himself from a life of crime, violence, and death.

Amelia

A twenty-one-year-old college dropout and drug user, Amelia is similar in many ways to Miguel. She is smart, sensitive, independent, well-read, physically attractive, and sexually active. She enjoys having sex with Firebug but doesn't love him because he has "no heart, no soul, nothing to cling to." She also has sex with Spider in exchange for crack. She loves Miguel and wants to have sex with him, but he won't allow it because he's in love with Cristalena and he doesn't want to betray his friend Firebug.

When Miguel and Amelia eventually do wind up between the sheets and remain chaste, you get the feeling that sleeping with someone of the opposite sex without having intercourse is a new experience for them. Amelia, who always feels "alone" after Firebug falls asleep, yearns to know what it's like to "sleep beside a warm, caring human," instead of "some living corpse." Miguel leaves the bed proud of what he *didn't* do, and hopeful that it will be "this warm and cozy" when he sleeps with Cristalena for the first time.

Very different from her two sisters who got hooked on clothes, took cooking classes, and married in their twenties, Amelia was good at math and starred on the debate team. "A Latino girl with brains," she always questioned authority: "Girls thought I was snotty and strange, and guys avoided me. I ended up hanging with people nobody liked—junkies, winos, potheads, hookers."

At City College, Amelia fell in love with a Puerto Rican nationalist whose intelligence and range of knowledge she respected but who made her feel as if she wasn't a real woman because she was more into books and a career than a family and children. Perhaps because her family had also been telling her this for most of her life, Amelia's self-esteem hit rock bottom, she dropped out of school, tuned in to Firebug and Spider, and turned on to crack.

When she meets Miguel through Firebug, Amelia recognizes the intelligence and sensitivity that sets him apart from the other kids in Spider's posse and tries to convince the teenager to abandon the drug trade: "Think about tomorrow," she tells him. "Gotta know when to cut out. Even Spider's countin' the days on one hand. Someday soon he'll tip. Just like a poof. Wha'chu gonna do with your life then?"

Because questions of this kind threaten his view of the world he'd like to believe he's living in and because he's not used to a woman speaking to him like an equal, Miguel continually shifts the focus from Amelia's concerns about his well-being to attacking her as a person. He frequently tells her, for example, that a college dropout who gets high on crack is too confused to know what she's talking about. Nevertheless, he can't deny that she has "figured him out and knows all the answers." As she guides Miguel away from self-deception and toward self-awareness, Amelia also goes through a transformation. She realizes she can't depend on a man to make her feel good about herself and resolves to do what she needs to do to be the person she wants to be: give up drugs and go back to school.

Cristalena

Sixteen-year-old Cristalena, whose name means "Christ's little one," is Miguel's other agent of redemption. This mostly good Latina girl lives at home, goes to high school, does her homework, and works part-time in a dress shop. Something of a guilt-ridden rebel as well, she wears lipstick and tight jeans when her religious parents aren't around, uses her more secular aunt as a cover to date boys, and initiates the first sexual encounter between herself and Miguel. Cristalena would also like to rid her neighborhood of all its drug dealers, which is why Miguel abandons his gold neck chains, leather jacket, and other beat-boy garb until he can find a way to tell her the truth about himself.

Cristalena is practical too. Realistic about her age, the importance of an education, and the necessity of a career, she's not about to hook up with a drug runner no matter how much she may love him. If Miguel is serious about their relationship, he is the one who will have to change. And he does. As Cristalena inspires Miguel to abandon the drug business, live at home, and go back to school, however, she also makes a change: she stops deceiving her parents. She tells them she is going to live the life she wants to live the way she wants to live it.

Catarina

Miguel's mom, Catarina, is one of only three women in *Spidertown*—Amelia and Cristalena are the others—to find any degree of happiness. All the rest make up a small army of mostly faceless, interchangeable, and easily disposed of sexual commodities who submit to the men in their lives without receiving any of the benefits of being protected and provided for. This is the way life is in the drug barrio. Because the women who run with Spider & Co. do not subscribe to the conventional definition of a good Latina girl—that is, a woman who places her man, her children, and her family above any of her individual needs—they open themselves up to subjugation, exploitation, and oppression. And in the eyes of the men who participate in the drug economy, they deserve everything that happens to them. What's sadly ironic about this is that the crack-addicted prostitutes in Rodriguez's novel play almost the same submissive, passively dutiful roles on the street that they would had they been married and living conventional lives in apartments.

The difference between these two groups of women, of course, is that the prostitutes have to hand over any money they earn to the pimps who supply them with the drugs they have become addicted to. As the price for drugs rises and their addictions inevitably grow stronger, the prostitutes have to take on more customers. This means charging lower and lower fees for their services. It isn't long before they can't afford to maintain a decent place to live, and until they turn themselves in to a detox center, are arrested by the police, or die of a drug overdose. They suffer the universal disrespect of the communities in which they live.

Because Catarina is content in the more respectable, subordinate role of Nelo's partner, she is more accepting than Amelia and Cristalena of the conventions imposed on her by the male-dominated culture. Miguel, who buys into the misogynistic social structure of his patriarchal culture, despises his mother for her sexual involvement with a series of men after his father abandoned the family. When Catarina brings one of these men, Nelo, home to live with them, Miguel blames her for his own abandonment and subsequent life as a drug runner. What struggles she may have had to endure as the female head of their household never enter his head. And while Nelo is genuinely interested in Catarina's happiness and doesn't beat her, he also insists on the respect accorded traditional patriarchal authority. Catarina confirms this when she tells her son that, if he wants to move back home, "You'll have to respect him, treat him like the man of the family."

Nelo is definitely the man. He doesn't let Catarina forget it, and he makes sure her son doesn't forget it either. When Catarina objects to Miguel's decision to visit Cristalena at an inappropriate hour, Nelo tells her, "Let him go. He's a man, isn't he? You'd think he was your daughter." Catarina is stunned by Nelo's overriding her objection as well as the disrespectful attitude toward women he conveys by his tone

Spidertown: A Novel and "Baptism Under Fire"

of his voice. Nevertheless, she accepts her restricted place in the family's new hierarchy. Miguel, of course, accepts Nelo's pronouncement and his mom's acquiescence without question or comment. Any extent to which his consciousness is raised will be determined by his independent minded, educationally ambitious, career-oriented girlfriend Cristalina and the intellectually independent, culturally uninhibited, outspoken feminist Amelia.

Spider

A recurring character, Spider is the same teenage drug runner who lures Angel from "Birthday Boy" into his web of crime. In *Spidertown* he has connected his filament to Joey and Yolanda from "Roaches" as well as Ritchie, Joyboy, and Willyboy from "Subway King." And as he did with Angel, he snares Miguel before he graduates from junior high. Only now, Spider is running his share of a drug enterprise along the lines of a U.S. corporation. Proud of his ability to grab ten-year-old kids off the street and turn them into successful businessmen faster than IBM, this would-be drug king's ambition is nothing less than providing access to the American Dream for those from whom it has been historically denied because of their ethnicity and class.

Spider also sees the underground economy he is forging as a social revolution, a street culture of youth resistance that beats capitalism at its own game. By providing well-paying jobs and multiple perks such as cars, guns, and women to unskilled workers and then training them for management positions complete with business cards with appropriately vague titles, Spider believes the level of financial security they attain will restore the sense of family unity that has been torn apart by the very drugs his minions are selling. In fact, there are whole families already working for him. Moreover, Spider hopes that he will be able to use his runners to create among young whites from the suburbs a new attitude toward Puerto Ricans, whose "poor is cool" style of dress and talk they will want to imitate in the same way they currently mimic African-American gangster rap artists. It's just a matter of getting the word out.

And who in Spider's world is in a better position to start him on the road to immortality than his former wanna-be writer and current lieutenant-in-waiting? In a tape recorded for the best-selling biography he imagines Miguel writing, Spider envisions the mega-movie that will follow and his subsequent appearance in a three-piece suit on *The Phil Donahue Show*: "The idea, Phil, is to inculcate in the youth the idea that they too can have big cars and guns and be Clint Eastwood and say make my day and have Robin Leach interview them while they lounge on their divan with a few blond beach bunnies. It's my job to open the world to them, to introduce them to the concept of business, free enterprise."

That managing a socioeconomic revolution of national proportions may require some black eyes, a few broken ribs, and even the death of an associate from time to time is a regrettable but necessary occupational hazard. It comes with the territory. "Maybe I do things a lo bruto sometimes... but these things gotta be done," Spider tells Miguel after having the tires on his car slashed. "it's like a big corporation thing. Like Exxon, Mobil Oil. You cross the corporation, thass it."

Rodriguez realized the character of Spider by hanging out

for eight months with the posse run by a twenty-eight-year-old former school friend. The young men sold crack and got into a lot of trouble: Rodriguez saw three people get shot, and two of them died. Because his relationship with his friend did not end well, until he moved to Germany, Rodriguez feared that some of the posse's members would come after him. Nevertheless, he cites his time with the posse as "more of a bonding experience than I ever had with Puerto Ricans."

Firebug

Miguel's friend Firebug is a teenage arsonist whose father used to build bonfires in a vacant lot on Tinton Avenue for him and his brothers to jump over. He also used a hot stove to punish them. In grade school Firebug carried lighter fluid to set wads of paper on fire and toss them at his teachers. And his punishment for setting a classmate on fire? Probation and a month in detention. Now he makes his living burning down buildings for slum landlords who want a quick and easy way to get rid of tenants and use the insurance money they collect to renovate their apartments and charge higher rents. Hanging on the wall of the apartment that Firebug and Miguel share is one of the thousands of metal sheets featuring vinyl decals of potted flowers with shutters and windowsills put up by the city of New York to cover the broken windows of burned-out buildings facing the newly built Bruckner Expressway. Miguel stashes his savings behind the metal sheet because he claims he's not old enough to have his own bank account. Neither is Firebug.

When not planning or executing one of his "wienie roasts," Firebug is usually either getting stoned or having sex with Amelia, who doesn't love him because, in her mind, he's devoid of human emotion. "He's got no time for love or friends," she tells Miguel. "He's a kind of insect." Nevertheless, Amelia is willing to watch with Miguel the buildings Firebug sets on fire—"Take that Pop!" Firebug never stays to watch the buildings he burns because he thinks it would be "bad luck," but he looks forward to meeting Amelia afterward and listening to her fan the flames of his ego with her vivid descriptions of the chaos his peculiar art has caused.

Firebug may not have much to offer Amelia, but in his own way he proves to be something of a friend to Miguel. When Miguel runs away from home and is forced to survive on the streets of El Bronx, Firebug introduces him to Spider, who recognizes the boy's potential for success, finds him an apartment, and begins grooming him for a top-level position in the drug business. When Miguel thinks about leaving Spider's organization, Firebug warns him of the streetwise veteran's vindictive nature and puts himself at risk of retaliation when he gives his friend a gun to protect himself. "Jus' you watch yuh back," he tells Miguel before exiting their apartment for another wienie roast.

Not Your Usual Generation Gap

Except for one scene, all the action in *Spidertown* takes place within the very small world of the South Bronx. And though it is recounted toward the end of the book, that scene takes place before the action of the novel begins. Miguel, Firebug, Amelia, and several of their friends are enjoying the day at Orchard Beach, a public beach in the Bronx: "Orchard Beach the shining star of the Caribbean, smell that sand

Spidertown: A Novel and "Baptism Under Fire"

surf chuletas lechon bacalaitos frying on the blackened grills in pots filled with bubbling oil, fat lady in a big white hat handing out tostones is if they were Bible tracts, every radio going full blast, kiddies scooting sand flying."

Orchard Beach cannot compare with any beach in Puerto Rico, but that doesn't stop the adults from reenacting the kind of cookouts they enjoyed when they lived on the island. Of course, the teenagers, with their overt sexual behavior and blatant use of marijuana, don't identify with their elders' nostalgia. And Firebug doesn't help matters when he accidentally blows up one of the adults' barbeques on wheels. For the kids, the sight of ribs and burgers strewn over the beach is funny. For the adults, it's no joke. Their day of reminiscing has been ruined.

This scene highlights some of the differences that can separate almost any two generations of people, but it also underscores a unique gap of understanding that exists between young Nuyoricans and their immigrant elders. Miguel and his friends have never been to Puerto Rico. They can't imagine what the adults transplanted from the island are reliving when they turn Orchard Beach into "The shining star of the Caribbean." Similarly, the adults can't recognize the kids' alienation from their island culture or why they ignore it. For them, the teenagers are simply crude and disrespectful.

What both groups need is a lesson in history. Even though the adults are part of the huge wave of immigration that took place after World War II, they don't fully understand the larger socioeconomic forces that brought them to New York. But rather than rebel against the hardships they endure, they escape by burying their heads in the sands of nostalgia. The teenagers, on the other hand, have no sense of how America's imperialist past affects their current barrio realities. This point is made clear by Rodriguez's use of the "The Shining Star" image that symbolized the supposed mutually beneficial partnership that was created when Puerto Rico became an American commonwealth in 1952. The result of that agreement, of course, is nothing to laugh about. It left Puerto Ricans born on the island open to decades of capitalist abuse and their children born in New York in a similar situation without a national identity. They're not Puerto Ricans because they're not from Puerto Rico, and they're not Americans because they've been denied access to opportunities available to citizens of the dominant white culture.

The State of Statelessness

During a discussion about how they should identify themselves, Miguel says he thinks of himself as "Latino." Cristalena tells him "Nah. You're a Puerto Rican American." She then informs him of the conventional classifications: "Hispanic is too much Spain. Latin American means Latin America. Puerto Rican American means you come from Puerto Rico." But he will accept none of them: "I know my identity. I'm a spick. I like spick, okay? It tells me right away what I am. It don't confuse me into thinkin' I'm American. I'm a spick, okay? Thass how whites see you anyway."

Miguel's choice of the demeaning word "spick"—from "No spicka de English"—reveals his position as someone who is caught between two nationalities. He is influenced by the material trappings of success that are touted in Amer-

Spidertown: A Novel and "Baptism Under Fire"

ican action films and advertisements, for example, but he does not aspire to be American. Nor is he interested in preserving his island heritage. As a "spick," Miguel sees himself on the lowest level of the country's class structure, a nobody whose prospects do not extend beyond the streets he cruises in his pimpmobile.

Miguel confirms his sense of insignificance when Spider fantasizes about which actor will play him in the movie that will come from the biography he wants the boy to write: "We want a Latino brother. Blacks got they own expression, now wham sayin'? We should have our own." Miguel replies that there are no Latino actors: "Not in Hollywood." To think that anyone in the American mainstream culture would be interested in reading a book or seeing a movie about "spicks" makes as much sense to Miguel as calling people like him and Spider "Hispanic," "Latin American," or even "Puerto Rican American."

Yet, Miguel and Spider do use the word "Latino" as a catch-all for the many displaced Puerto Ricans, Cubans, Dominicans, and Mexicans inhabiting the state of concentrated poverty that constitutes El Bronx. Few, if any, Puerto Ricans anywhere refer to themselves as "Puerto Rican Americans." An increasing number, regardless of where they were born, use the word *Boricua* as an expression of social and political solidarity. It's the name the island went by before it was colonized by the United States.

Perhaps the word that best expresses the identity of the deculturated people who populate Rodriguez's novels and short stories has yet to be invented, and when it is, it may well be a combination of English and Spanish. Rodriguez's characters, like the people of the South Bronx and other Puerto Rican communities in the Northeast United States, use both languages when they speak—"Maybe I do things a lo bruto sometimes." They also use words common to African-American speech: "Yo bro, long time I don't flesh it up with my piece, know wham sayin'?" Whatever current word best describes Rodriguez's "lowercase people," the language they speak reinforces their location on the outermost fringes of American culture: citizens in name only.

The Language That Crosses All Boundaries

Miguel, Amelia, Detective Sanchez, and Spider distinguish themselves from the other characters in *Spidertown* by their shared interest in reading. Miguel uses books to escape, Amelia to learn, Sanchez to instruct, and Spider to inflate his ego and motivate others. Miguel grew up loving books. And he kept reading them in secret long after his father, who may have been threatened by the knowledge his son was gaining, started destroying any book brought into the house. He even dreamed about being a writer someday. That dream ended when Miguel thought he discovered there was no such thing as a Puerto Rican writer, but his love of books never diminished despite leaving school in the seventh grade and running away from home at the age of fourteen.

When his character is introduced, Miguel is sixteen and has stopped reading. Or so he says. "My father was right," he tells Amelia. "Lookit me now. The streets. Thass a education." Amelia doesn't believe a word he says, not with the more than one hundred books she has seen stacked in his room. She understands Miguel: "You're just mad now, and confused. I can see it. You don't belong on these streets doin' this. You're too sensitive. You're yearning for something better."

Miguel claims that books "don't lead nowhere," but he knows they bring him to places and introduce him to people beyond the constricting world of drugs, crime, and violence in El Bronx. The books on his shelves, mostly classics by authors such as Tolstoy, Dickens, and Mark Twain, are more than just vehicles of escape. They often focus their readers' attention on the plights of disadvantaged and oppressed people. Through books, Miguel discovers that Moscow, London, and the Mississippi Delta are not as far away from El Bronx as he may have thought.

Books also help Miguel understand himself and the world he lives in. He bonds with Spider when the two discuss Dickens's *Oliver Twist*, a novel about an innocent runaway who becomes ensnared in a life of street crime he doesn't have the stomach for. Spider has read it five times. Likening himself to Fagin, the adult leader of the boys in Dickens's novel, Spider asks Miguel if he sees himself as a kind of Oliver Twist: "Nah," Miguel says, rubbing his chin. "The Artful Dodger." Rubbing his chin is the key phrase here. Miguel is thinking about what to say. He may see himself as an innocent, victimized version of Oliver Twist, but he knows that's not the answer his mentor wants to hear. The rank of the Artful Dodger in Fagin's army of child criminals is what Spider would call a "lieutenant," the position he's grooming Miguel for and the position Miguel aspires to.

93

Lying to Spider because he wants to advance in the drug business shows that Miguel is learning his lessons well. Spider may know he's lying, but he doesn't care whether he is because in his mind Miguel is demonstrating loyalty to him by saying he's the kind of person Spider wants him to become. And for that the young boy is rewarded: "Spider looked pleased. . . . Then he picked up a blunt and lit it. 'Smoke with me, man.'"

Amelia is not so accepting when Miguel tries to play the same game with her, namely, saying whatever you need to say to get whatever it is you want. She also won't let Miguel get away with fooling himself into thinking he's got it made. Pointing out the disconnect between Jean-Paul Sartre's perspective on the importance of individual morally responsible choices and the drug economy of El Bronx, she tells Miguel, "I guess the whole thing is the biggest self-deception there is. Just look at this street, man. All these people . . . convincing themselves that it's life. Some people do it real good. The better you are at fooling yourself, the happier you'll be. Some people, they can't do it at all." Miguel, of course, is a pro at deceiving himself, so it will take more than Amelia's irrefutable logic and Sartre's existential philosophy to make him see the truth about his life as a drug runner. It will take his love for Cristalena, Spider's betrayal, and an author whose works he hasn't yet read: Richard Wright.

Detective Sanchez gives Miguel a copy of Wright's *Native Son* (1940) while the boy is recuperating in the hospital from Spider's attempt to kill him. Miguel likes the book—he awards it his highest compliment: "dope"—and he's a good enough reader to connect the dots linking him, Oliver Twist, and Wright's Bigger Thomas. All three char-

Spidertown: A Novel and "Baptism Under Fire"

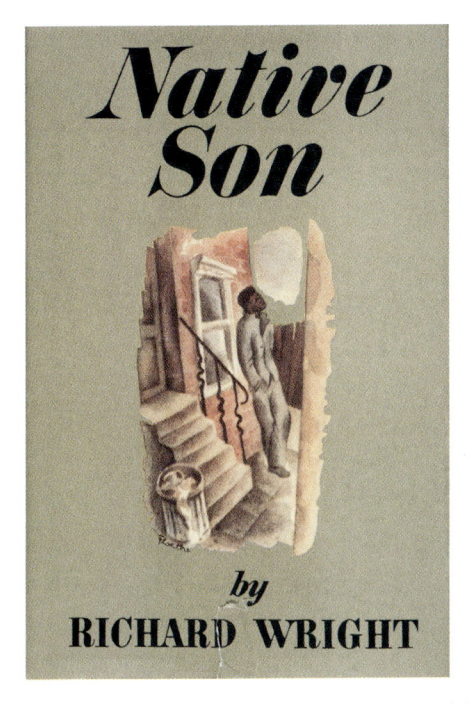

One of the three books that make the strongest impression on the young Miguel is Richard Wright's *Native Son*—a story of a black man in America that resonates with his own experience as a young Puerto Rican in New York City.

acters are caught in desperate worlds from which they wish to escape, but they can't free themselves or achieve a greater sense of awareness about their condition without the help of an older and wiser, father figure. For Oliver, that figure comes in the form of the wealthy Mr. Brownlow, who adopts him. For Bigger Thomas, it is his lawyer Mr. Max, and for Miguel, it is Detective Sanchez.

What he likes about Wright, Sanchez tells Miguel, is "his ability to present us with the case of a young man who was born into a situation that he couldn't change. He couldn't help what he did. He just didn't know any better, and there was no one to teach him." What Miguel hears is that he's a good boy, he's not responsible for his behavior, he can make amends, and he can rely on Sanchez to guide him in the right direction.

Miguel begins his journey of redemption by burning

his beloved car—a symbol of his masculinity as well as his street status—and turning over to Sanchez the cassette tape on which Spider has recorded his life of crime. Miguel also learns that the plight of Puerto Ricans is not much different from those of African Americans. "Sometimes I feel like more Puerto Ricans should read it," the detective tells him. "We could learn so much from the black man." And should he think again about becoming a writer, Miguel could learn from Richard Wright as well. Perhaps even write a *Native Son* for Puerto Ricans.

As good a choice as *Native Son* is for Miguel, it's something of a puzzle why, in a novel that's loaded with allusions to books and writers, Rodriguez does not have Detective Sanchez give the boy a copy of Piri Thomas's *Down These Mean Streets*. Wouldn't it have been more meaningful for the Nuyorican Sanchez to have given the Nuyorican Miguel a book about a Nuyorican rather than a novel by an African American? Couldn't Miguel have learned as much from one as from the other?

Rodriguez has said in interviews that he was angry at Piri Thomas for not visiting his high school and encouraging young people to seek avenues of self-expression in the arts. He didn't know until much later that Thomas was in jail at the time. Nevertheless, the the absence of *Down These Mean Streets* in *Spidertown* might be seen as a kind of payback for what Rodriguez sees as Thomas's neglecting a younger generation of writers when he wasn't in prison. More than likely, it is a comment that Thomas's voice doesn't resonate with the new generation of readers whose language and levels of awareness are more like Rodriguez's.

Life as a Movie

Miguel's fascination with fiction doesn't end with books: "In the street-level war game of the crack trade, there are so many reasons for murdering someone than not that it's a miracle that bodies don't have to be pushed off lots by bulldozers like in all those classic black-and-whites of the forties." His allusion to old gangster movies and his description of bodies being pushed by bulldozers in newsreels about the Holocaust are two of several images appearing in the novel that measure the extent to which Miguel's life has been influenced by the cinema.

Like books, movies enable Miguel to escape, but he doesn't use them primarily to take him to places where he can experience the times, cultures, and lives of people different from his own. He uses them instead to inspire movies in his mind and, by running them continually in his imagination, turn the "street-level war game of the crack trade" into an adventure: "What a movie life to be standing on the street one minute sharing a joke and the next to find yourself frozen staring for a fraction of a second at a car that slows, at a gun muzzle poking from the back seat through the open window."

A rugged individualist, a war hero of the streets, a survivor who has to maintain his guard against an enemy that can change from week to week, Miguel readily buys into Spider's fantasy about giving kids like him an opportunity to imagine they're playing a movie role the same way Clint Eastwood would. Only Miguel, being a cut above most other kids his age, prefers to be seen as the more innocent, victimized but equally tough hero created by Marlon Brando in *On the Waterfront*. A seasoned veteran of urban guerrilla

Marlon Brando's famous line as Terry Malloy in *On the Waterfront* was "I coulda been a contender." Miguel identifies very strongly with the character, the situation, and the sentiments.

wars at sixteen, Miguel withstands the brutal intimidation of corrupt police officers, a horrific beating by Ritchie and his posse, and two bullets in his back.

Cristalena warns Miguel that his life as a drug runner "ain't no movie," but he's so unable or unwilling to distinguish fact from fantasy he can't help but see even their romance through a war perspective. A good example of this occurs when Miguel waits for Amelia to get out of work at the dress shop: "He leaned against a parked car and waited,

Spidertown: A Novel and "Baptism Under Fire"

out of sight of the storefront so he couldn't be spotted. An ambush, he thought to himself, grinning."

Miguel's cinematic mind also plays with varying images of his own murder: "machine gun slugs ripping through the car, windshield punctured with holes, glass flying around him like dust." As long as nothing is real, or only as real as what you see in a movie, nothing has to be feared. Bullets don't hurt; they excite. Victims aren't people; they're nerds too stupid to know how to protect themselves. Nobody dies; they just get "mushroomed": "It's like being in a war movie and hugging your wounded buddy, like being in a war movie and escaping by the skin of your teeth and then staring at each other in the cold, laughing, wiping at wet eyes and feeling crazy grateful."

Mimicking characters in movies is not the only example of life imitating art in *Spidertown*. Miguel mimics the Artful Dodger from *Oliver Twist*, Spider mimics a successful capitalist with a humanitarian mission on the talk show *Donahue*, he and Firebug mimic behavior suggested by their names, immigrants at a beach in the Bronx mimic what their lives were like on beaches in Puerto Rico, and vinyl decals installed by the city to cover up the windows in burned-out buildings mimic the real flowers and shuttered windows of houses that people actually live in. The list goes on and on. Perhaps the South Bronx, with its mindless violence, loveless sex, and recreational drugs is not as far from the cultural mainstream as it first appears. Perhaps in their attempt to mimic what has been marketed to them as entertainment, many of Rodriguez's drug runners really do believe they are living the American Dream.

Abraham Rodriguez

Machoman in Crisis

The star of the movie he continually runs in his mind, Miguel uses the cinematic images he creates to confirm his idea of himself as macho. To be macho is to be more than just male. It is to prize such activities as drinking, taking risks, standing your ground, hating gay people, and demeaning women. Its motto is "Loyalty." Firebug is a good example. When not burning down buildings, he's mostly stoned on drugs or engaged in screaming sex fests with women. Sometimes both. His conversation is often laced with homophobic pronouncements, and he touts the sexual superiority of Latin males over white ones. He enjoys the camaraderie of men who see the world the same way he does and is loyal to them as well. When Miguel considers pulling out of the drug business, Firebug cautions him against throwing away a career, warns him of Spider's vindictive nature, and possibly puts his own life at risk with Spider when he provides his friend with a gun.

Miguel, for his part, is also pretty macho. He stands his ground when a white officer who has been corrupted by bribes puts a gun in his face and demonstrates his sense of loyalty when he refuses to have sex with Firebug's girlfriend Amelia. Miguel has another, more sensitive side, however. He reads—an activity he denies in public because the type of macho men he associates with consider it feminine. He also cries when he is alone and fears Cristalena might leave him.

Miguel's adherence to macho codes of behavior is encouraged and rewarded by Spider, a surrogate father for a lot of the boys in his posse who've run away from home because their real fathers abused them. Miguel's father,

Spidertown: A Novel and "Baptism Under Fire"

for example, beat him, and Firebug's father left scars from a burning stove on the boy's body as punishment for misbehaving. Interestingly, Spider's father never abused him, but in his mind the man who worked for the post office for twenty years only to spend his retirement playing dominos on a streetcorner is little more than a chump. Spider wants more out of life. To get it, he chooses the easiest and most lucrative path available to him in El Bronx: the drug trade. But success in this business sometimes requires administering a kind of "discipline" not usually found in a post office.

Violence, including the deaths of some of the youngsters who view him as a father figure, is part of the territory. Firebug understands this: "Business is business," he tells Miguel after Spider allowed him to be bloodied by Ritchie and the boys in his posse. But Miguel doesn't understand. "What about friendship?" he asks. To which Firebug replies, "Spider's still yuh friend, bro'. You got the wrong attitude. . . . I'm sure you'll see in a couple a days . . . tha' maybe you deserved a beatin'."

Until he meets Cristalena, Miguel adheres to the codes that typify social relationships among most macho males. When he decides to get out of the drug business, however, Spider questions the boy's loyalty. His wish to live with his parents, return to school, love Cristalena, and experience the life of a normal sixteen-year-old violates the masculine codes Miguel is expected to live by. As a consequence, the boy is forced to suffer the withdrawal of Spider's protection, the loss of his status as lieutenant-in-training, the intimidation of corrupt police officers, the slashing of his car tires, and the brutal beating by Ritchie and his posse. When these tactics fail to bring Miguel back to the fold, Spider sets up his protégé to die in a drive-by shooting at a busy nightclub called Spadgies.

Miguel is wounded as much by Spider's attacks on his sense of loyalty as he is by the assassin's bullets, but after the shooting he feels as if he's the one who has been betrayed: "I thought 'chu was really my pana," he tells Spider. "But 'chu jus' lookin' out f' yuhself, Spider . . . . I can't work f' you, f' anybody like that." Any action Miguel takes now is for his own survival. And because he kept his appointment to meet Spider at the bar where the shooting took place, his mentor can no longer question his loyalty. Accompanied by his redemptive agents Cristalena and Amelia, he burns his car—a symbol of masculinity and status—and turns over to Detective Sanchez the incriminating tape on which Spider has recorded his life of crime. Now, under the guidance of a new father figure, Miguel can reenter the conventional world he left behind when he joined Spider's posse.

Women as Agents of Change

They're not faster than a speeding bullet, more powerful than a locomotive, or able to leap tall buildings in a single bound, but Amelia and Cristalena are certainly superwomen. Unlike Miguel's mom, they don't submit to patriarchal authority, and unlike all the other women in the novel, they are not reduced to interchangeable, disposable sexual objects. Not only do they successfully resist the challenges of their misogynist culture, they serve as feminist catalysts of change for Miguel. No mean feat in a world where submission to patriarchy is the law. Rodriguez writes, "In the world Miguel'd grown up in you start with backyards and rubble lots and then you conquer girls. You get your way with them and you learn that's the way, in life you are supposed to get your way. The woman is supposed to know where she's at, where she BELONGS. It was all in his blood. To be THE MAN. The woman just did what the man said. That was respect. Tradition."

Amelia may be Firebug's girlfriend, but she is Miguel's soul mate. Intelligent, independent, resilient, and resourceful, she creates her own definition of what it means to be a woman. She holds down a job in a community where there are few opportunities for employment, maintains her own apartment, speaks her mind, doesn't defer to anyone, rejects the traditionally submissive roles embraced by her older sisters, and engages in sex with whomever she wants whenever she wants for whatever reasons she wants.

Because she has dropped out of college and started using crack, Miguel at first writes Amelia off as someone with brains but no common sense. Still, he can't resist the logic of her arguments. Criticizing Spider's skewed vision of the American Dream, she tells Miguel: "Self-deception. We get some money an' it buys us VCRs an' stereos an' gold chains an' we drive through the streets shooting at each other like we're big bad successful men. But it's a trap. White people couldn't a' come up with a better way to screw up blacks an' Latinos."

Nor does Amelia soften the truth when it comes to deflating Miguel's view of Spider. About the boy's father figure, she says, "What happens when he leaves the ghetto? Ain't he nothing once he steps out of this place? . . . You go out into the real world, that's someone else's turf. You can be a big man on Fox Street, but once you head downtown you're just another ugly spick kid." And not for a minute will she allow Miguel to think he's not partially responsible for the impact drugs have on the El Bronx community: "If I wanna destroy myself, it's my right, do you hear? I ain't out to destroy anyone else. Unlike you. . . . Go ahead, act like you care about someone other than yourself."

Perhaps because he has begun to have some second thoughts of his own about the drug business, Miguel listens to what Amelia has to say even while he mounts personal attacks against her. She doesn't let him get away with these either: "Sixteen, but able to hurt women as well as any adult man. Congratulations."

If only Amelia wasn't so smart, so well-read, and so right all the time. If only she didn't know so much about drugs, sex, and crime. If only she wasn't so independent and outspoken, Miguel might be more attracted to her. But this boy still has a way to go on the road of feminist consciousness before he can fully appreciate a woman like Amelia. How far he has to travel might be measured in his relationship with Cristalena.

Here's how Amelia describes Cristalena: "Sounds like some kinda dishwashing liquid. . . . Straight, virginal, innocent, clean. Goes to church. . . . a little virgin, a device sent by heaven to cleanse your soul." A younger and quieter rebel than Amelia or Miguel, Cristalena wages her own battle for independence against her Pentecostal parents' oppressive gender conventions. Deception is her weapon of choice. She changes into fashionable clothes at school and meets any boys she wishes to date at her aunt's apartment. She even pursues Miguel aggressively and initiates their first sexual encounter. She falls in love and wants to live with Miguel, but not if he has anything to do with drugs and not at the expense of her reputation. She also takes her education seriously. It's her ticket out of the barrio and into a career: "I ain't tying myself to some sinking ship," she tells Miguel. "I know that sounds cold, but I got plans."

And Miguel wants to be included. He stops wearing gold chains, abandons his sexual conquests of women and becomes monogamous, and learns from Cristalena that being macho in a male-female relationship is not healthy behavior. He realizes that they must "respect each other," and he apologizes to her for trying to order her around.

Cristalena, in turn, finds the strength in her love for Miguel to stand up to her parents and tell them she is going to dress as she pleases and date whomever she likes. Able to rebel against gender conventions without jeopardizing her status as a good Latina girl—one who stands by her man—Miguel bestows upon her the diamond bracelet Spider told him to save for "some real girl someday."

The "real girl" Cristalena and the almost surreal woman Amelia become friends and combine forces to help Miguel escape from Spider's drug enterprise. They are with him in the hospital when he recovers from gunshot wounds, when he burns his car, and when he hands over to Detective Sanchez the tape that will incriminate Spider. At the novel's end, Miguel, Cristalena, and Amelia walk arm in arm away from a setting sun into a future with a lot of promise and no posses.

This seems an unlikely ending for a story by Abraham Rodriguez. Sanchez gets his man, Amelia goes back to school, Miguel and Cristalena live happily ever after? The good guys win, and Spider's days outside of prison are numbered? With the exception of the short story "The Boy Without a Flag," Rodriguez has been relentlessly uncompromising in his bleak view of life in El Bronx. He may have softened slightly with his characterizations of Miguel, Cristalena, and Amelia, but to allow Miguel to walk out of Spider's web with the two change agents by his side and only the scars from a couple of bullet holes in his back makes *Spidertown* sound less like a novel that confronts harsh reality as it is experienced everyday in the barrio and more like a fairy-tale romance. No wonder Hollywood is interested.

"Baptism Under Fire"

Three years after the events in *Spidertown*, Miguel and Cristalena appear in Rodriguez's "Baptism Under Fire," which was published in the *Sycamore Review* in 1997. The former drug runner is now a mail clerk, and the former student with her eyes set on a career in fashion is now pregnant. He has become more domesticated—he cooks, if badly—but is still macho enough to bully Cristalena into eating what she doesn't like. Because she's still a good Latina girl, Cristalena downs so much of Miguel's poorly prepared food he feels guilty about forcing her. But he's not guilty enough to help her with her prenatal breathing exercises or time her contractions. Having a baby is her job.

Cristalena wants to name their baby "Gigi" because she is sure it will be a girl, and Miguel, equally sure it will be a boy, wants to call the baby "Ramon." They fight about this until four in the morning, but once they are able to share their fears as they did in *Spidertown*, they make up in words that demonstrate Miguel's continued preoccupation with viewing his life as if he were a character in a never-ending action film: "It was like in the war movie where the veteran turns back to the weepy kid and says 'Hell, we're all scared, kid.'" Pretending that he's living a movie, as he did in *Spidertown*, may be an effective way for Miguel to make sense of his life, or it may be a way for him to make it bearable, but it comes across in "Baptism Under Fire" as an immature way for a young man about to be a father to respond to his wife's concerns.

Miguel is no longer the "baby" Amelia said he was in *Spidertown*, but he hasn't quite crossed the threshold of adulthood either. The nurse in "Baptism Under Fire" refers to him as a "half grownup," and it's easy to see why from the counterproductive ways he responds to her, the hospital security guard, and one of the doctors. It's also easy to see why Miguel is so angry about no one believing he's old enough to be Cristalena's husband and why he continues to feel so alienated from people of his own culture. His wife, meanwhile, has her baby girl without his being there.

The story ends with Miguel seeing an image of himself in the way his newborn daughter behaves: "A scared, twitching baby, punching at the air, screaming to high heaven, forever waiting to be carefree and embraced. And at that moment Miguel knew more about his life than he had, ever." At the same moment, the new father reveals again a character trait that has been a large part of who he is since the earliest pages of *Spidertown*: for Miguel, there isn't much that happens in his life that isn't all about Miguel.

The Buddha Book is thematically similar to the earlier books of Abraham Rodriguez, but the format contains elements of graphic novels.

5

THE BUDDHA BOOK: A NOVEL AND *SOUTH BY SOUTH BRONX*

I'm not angry. I was never angry. I just feel strongly about things. The passion is real.

—Abraham Rodriguez

The Buddha Book: A Novel

The Buddha Book: A Novel covers much of the same territory as *The Boy Without a Flag* and *Spidertown*: dysfunctional family conflicts, women with minds of their own, macho men, authority figures trying to maintain control, youngsters at war with themselves, the current status of America's colonial agenda, and the devastating effects of drugs on the "lowercase people" of El Bronx. There's even a cameo appearance by his novel, *Spidertown*. Why the repetition? Rodriguez tells us: "In my eyes, this community never faced its failure in terms of dealing with its youth. And now it wants to bury the past by paving over it." Rodriguez is simply not going to allow this to happen. Determined to hold accountable those responsible for the tragedy that is the

Abraham Rodriguez

South Bronx, he exposes their abuses in every story he tells.

The Buddha Book opens with a murder. Jose loses his temper and drowns his ex-girlfriend Lucy in her bathtub because she has dumped him for the drug dealer Angel, whom Rodriguez introduced to readers in "The Birthday Boy." A newcomer to crime, Jose is guilt-ridden by what he has done and searches for a way to confess to the murder for which there are no witnesses. He finds what he's looking for in *The Buddha Book*, an underground comic book that he and his friend Dinky, like Edwin and the character Rodriguez in "The Boy Without a Flag," have been writing, illustrating, printing, and distributing to the kids in their high school. Featuring true stories with actual names about the mostly aimless liaisons that take place among the teachers, staff, and students at their high school, each issue irritates the school's authorities. Together, the boys decide to print a final issue of *The Buddha Book* that tells the story of Lucy's murder and serves as a confession for Jose.

In addition to Jose and Dinky, a reluctant drug runner who wants to keep his younger brothers out of the business his incarcerated father is unsuccessfully pressuring the boy to maintain, there is a third main character. Jose's stepsister Anita is a stripper, Angel groupie, and murderer whose sole ambition is to gain notoriety as the world's first Puerto Rican female serial killer. She even pulls a gun on her friend Dinky to force him to have sex with her. The boy is not altogether unwilling, but he does worry about getting shot. A reversal of the many scenes in popular movies, books, and television shows in which the man is usually the one who forces the woman to have sex, Rodriguez may want his readers to admire the bold action taken by Anita.

Some critics have pointed to Dinky, Jose, and Anita as negative portraits of Puerto Ricans, but Rodriguez claims they are not: "They are intelligent, resourceful young people, who as usual have to face immensely difficult decisions with no one around to offer guidance or even support. My characters make decisions, good ones. Jose decides not to get away with his crime, and Dinky decides to not follow the path laid out by his forefathers. Anita sees nothing and creates from that her own unique career." There is no doubt that Rodriguez's characters are intelligent and resourceful and, in the case of Dinky, positively portrayed. But Jose and Anita are murderers. Rodriguez may succeed in making his readers care about them as people, but does that mean any moral stance taken toward their behavior should be ambiguous?

Both murderers want to get away with their crimes, but they also want to be caught: —Jose to embarrass his wannabe principal stepfather as well as to assuage his guilt—and Anita for the publicity her trial will bring. She can't wait to see herself on television: "The leading female serial killer of note should rate at least twenty minutes with maybe some footage." At least Anita expects to be punished for her crime. Jose, though he regrets having murdered Lucy, imagines himself being absolved for his murder by a lawyer who will portray him as the victim, a "Puerto Rican geek kid driven mad by high-performance high school life and the pressures of society spoon-feeding him violence on TV until he just had to go out and prove it by killing a girl who only enters the story parenthetically."

In the same way that Rodriguez balances Jose's murder with Dinky's decision to get out of the drug business and protect his younger brothers from entering it, Rodriguez balances Anita's multiple murders with the behavior of a woman whose responses to her environment mark positive contributions to her families and her community: Dinky's mother stops drinking and works to protect her sons from their father's drug operation.

What most separates *The Buddha Book* from *Spidertown* is its ending. Rodriguez doesn't allow this novel's three teenage protagonists a fairy-tale escape. Instead of walking them away from the barrio toward a future beyond the borders of El Bronx, he walks them into the local police precinct. And it's no coincidence that he uses almost the exact same words in the concluding lines of each book. *Spidertown* ends with "There was only the three of them, walking away from it," and *The Buddha Book* ends with "There was only the three of them. This time walking right into it."

"This time" are the telling words here. An obvious reference to and retraction from his position in *Spidertown*, Rodriguez affirms what for him has been an almost continuous message since he completed his short story "The Boy Without a Flag": there is no escape from the terrifying effects the drug economy has on young people growing up in the South Bronx. Nor for readers of Rodriguez's other stories is there any escape from the barrio, which plays as much of a role as one of his characters, many of whom appear in more than one fiction. For this reason, *The Buddha Book* often seems weighed down by what has preceded it. At the same time, much seems left out. Rodriguez's narrator notes, for example, that the much-anticipated final edition of *The Buddha Book* is greeted with a standing ovation, but he doesn't tell us much about the impact on its readers.

Similarly, Rodriguez doesn't convey his characters' motives as thoroughly as he did in *Spidertown*. On the other hand, he may have intended Dinky, Jose, and Anita to be perceived as the kind of caricatures that often appear in comic books. They come close, and the book's graphically illustrated cover suggests as much. And what, in the final analysis, does *The Buddha Book* have to do with Buddhism? Though "Buddha" is used as another name for marijuana in the novel, Rodriguez notes: "The Buddhists say if you don't get it right this time, you gotta come back and do it again, from the beginning." Perhaps this is why Rodriguez keeps repeating so many of the same themes with so many of the same characters.

South by South Bronx

South by South Bronx places Rodriguez's familiar view of ghetto life within the larger context of international intrigue. He also brings back the ever-ready and willing Detective Sanchez to serve as one of the novel's two narrators. Only now, the good police officer from *Spidertown* and "Roaches" may have proved himself to be too good for his own good. His fellow officers shun him because he reported a vigilante cop who decided to take the law into his own hands and kill some of the hoodlums the courts failed to put in jail. Disloyalty, Sanchez discovers, is almost as big an offense in the macho world of police officers as it is in the drug business. If he ever needs

SOUTH BY SOUTH BRONX

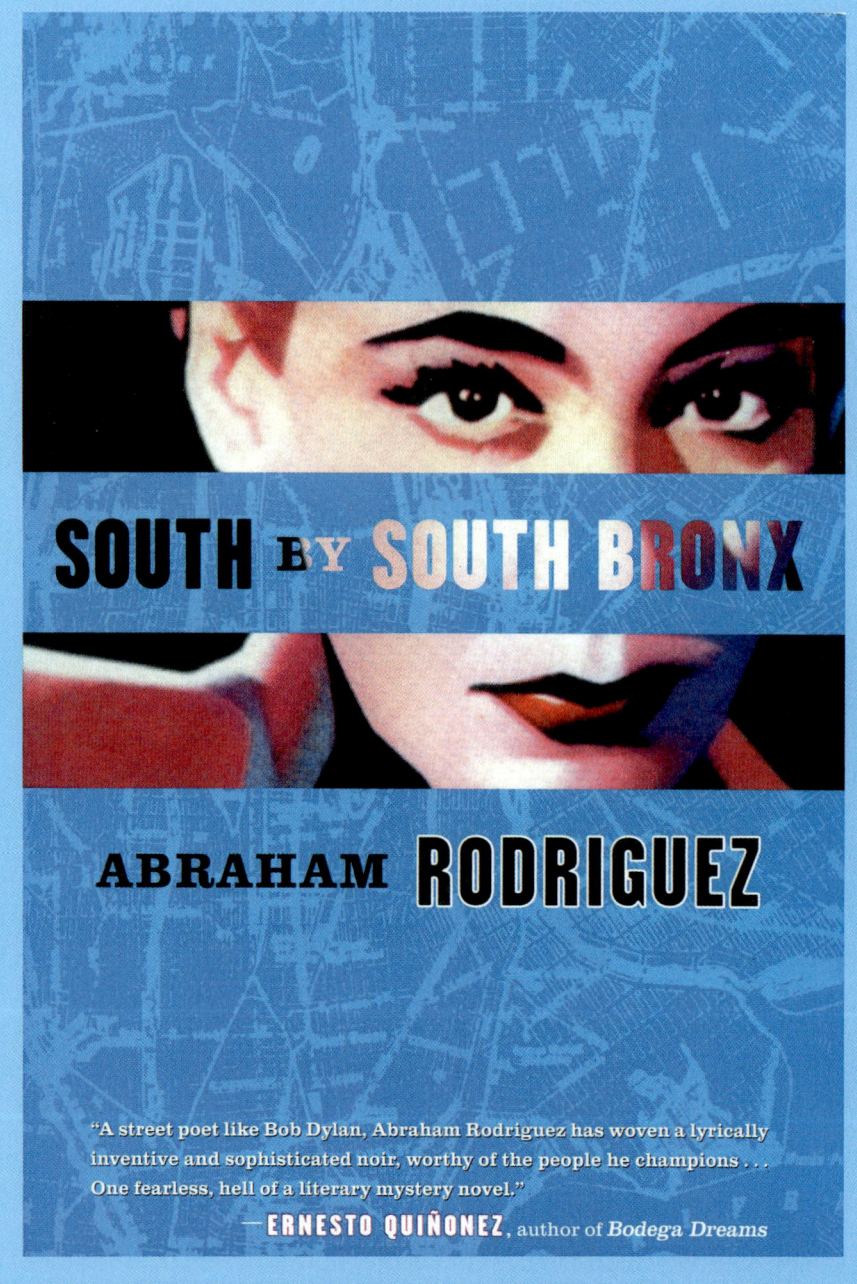

ABRAHAM RODRIGUEZ

"A street poet like Bob Dylan, Abraham Rodriguez has woven a lyrically inventive and sophisticated noir, worthy of the people he champions... One fearless, hell of a literary mystery novel."
—ERNESTO QUIÑONEZ, author of *Bodega Dreams*

A post 9/11 novel, *South by South Bronx* places Rodriguez's familiar themes in an international context.

to call for backup, he can't be confident that anyone from his precinct will cover his back. Or even show up.

The novel opens with alcoholic shoe salesman Alex waking up to discover a beautiful blond woman in his bed. He assumes she is the result of another of his increasingly frequent blackouts. But Ava Reynolds is no one-night stand. She also packs a pistol.

In the months before 9/11, Arab terrorists funneled $10 million to a drug dealer named Spook in the South Bronx. The money was supposed to pay off local politicians and law enforcement officers, but it seems Spook took off with it instead. Now everyone from the terrorists to the FBI is after him.

Ava Reynolds was with Spook's brother David when they were shot at, and she climbed the nearest fire escape and jumped into the first open window she could find. She quickly and easily captivates the alcoholic Alex as well as his friends Mink and Monk. Mink is a once-successful painter, and Monk is a once critically acclaimed novelist. Ava brings both men out of their creative blocks, but it isn't long before Monk mysteriously disappears.

Enter Detective Sanchez. He thinks he is investigating a missing person, or possible homicide case until he is visited by federal agent Myers, who is searching for Spook, Spook's brother David, and the money they have apparently stolen from the terrorists. Myers wants Sanchez's help. It's Myers who has ordered his assistant Ava Reynolds to befriend the drug dealers and see if she can discover the whereabouts of the money. That's what she was doing when she and David were shot at. When Ava realizes Myers is looking to keep the $10 million for himself and that her life may be in as much danger as Spook's and David's, she decides to flee the country. But first she's got to get out of El Bronx. Alex, Mink, and Monk try to help her, but she is not nearly the victim she presents herself to be. In fact, Ava herself may have stolen the money. Or at least know where it is.

Nor is Sanchez the same cop he was in "Roaches" and *Spidertown*. Still able to identify with disenfranchised people of color and trying to do his job to the best of his ability, he battles daily with the temptation to make some money from the corruption that surrounds him. Now that he can no longer depend on his mostly white fellow officers to protect him, that $10 million would allow him to retire from the police force, get out of El Bronx, and save his life.

Does this all sound like a black-and-white crime film from the 1930s or 1940s? It would if it weren't for Rodriguez's familiar but significantly watered-down social criticism and the popular technique of shifting between two points of view, each identified by different typefaces. One narrative is told from the first person point of view of Sanchez; the other, told in the third person, follows the story of Alex, Ava, Mink, and Monk. "Some people were disoriented at first reading it," Rodriguez comments, "but already in my last book I was tired of the linear thing."

Another reason for reader confusion may be Rodriguez's decision to include photos and brief biographies of the actress Marlene Dietrich, the German filmmaker Leni Riefenstahl, and the poet Anne Sexton. If these women were intended to add depth by association to Ava, the novel's only central female character, he failed. A white woman from the

The Buddha Book: A Novel and South by South Bronx

A brief biography of Marlene Dietrich is included in *South by South Bronx*.

Upper East Side with a distinctive 1930s haircut, undeniable beauty, and a mysterious past, Ava never transcends her cinematic stereotype. Perhaps because writing about people who are not from El Bronx is new for Rodriguez, the mysterious blond Ava comes off as an almost one-dimensional caricature when compared with the powerful women in the other novels who share the same first letter of her name: Amelia in *Spidertown* and Anita in *The Buddha Book*.

117

Given the focus of his previous works, what's interesting about *South by South Bronx* is the degree to which Rodriguez has expanded his subject to include someone beyond the immediate confines of El Bronx. If only he had made Ava's relationship with the Puerto Rican men she meets more complicated, he might have expanded his readers' understanding of some of the people who live there. Or some of the ways people from El Bronx might view someone from the dominant culture. Rodriguez notes, "I see the world coming into the Bronx," but he gives no indication of what they learn from it or what others can learn from their being there. Ava disappears almost as mysteriously as she arrived.

What's also interesting about *South by South Bronx* is the degree to which Rodriguez has strayed from the paths that other writers, artists, and musicians working out of El Bronx have been following during the same period as he was writing his book. This is especially true of wall murals and hip-hop. These artists focus more on celebrating the diversity among Latinos, their triumphs over the crack economy, and the many ways the area's residents have resisted the influence and control of the dominant white culture.

Nevertheless, *South by South Bronx* is a significant artistic departure from what has preceded it. An obvious allusion to Alfred Hitchcock's film *North by Northwest* (1959), the opening of *South by South Bronx* is typical Hitchcockian fare. The acclaimed film director often opened his movies with a seemingly ordinary person suddenly being thrust into a confusing, often dangerous situation that all too quickly takes over his entire life. And how about the mysterious pistol-packing woman who shows up in Alex's bed bearing a name similar to that of Eva Marie Saint, the Hollywood actress who starred alongside Cary Grant in *North by Northwest*? Eva and Ava even share the same fashion-model look and enigmatic behaviors.

Perhaps *South by South Bronx*, then, does reflect to some degree the evolving condition of the South Bronx. It's certainly not the same place Rodriguez described when he began writing more than thirty years ago. And the same can be said of the characters he chooses to portray in his most recent novel. Perhaps reflecting the borough's recent renaissance in music and art, Mink is a painter and Monk is a writer. Even shoe salesman Alex is a far cry from the druggies, prostitutes, gang bangers, and teenage parents that inhabit Rodriguez's earlier fiction.

But something else is also missing: the explicit emphasis on corresponding social justice themes. It's as if Rodriguez's uncompromising depiction of the human condition as it is experienced in the South Bronx has given way almost completely to film mimicry. Could he have made a conscious decision to cinematize his narrative style so that it will be more appealing to Hollywood filmmakers, who generally do not show much interest in social justice issues?

Rodriguez has explored to a significant extent the theme of life imitating art in his earlier works. In writing *South by South Bronx*, he seems to be living it. Could it be that his best work is now behind him or, like the three main characters in his most successful novel *Spidertown*, will Rodriguez's full potential not be realized until he manages to escape from the limitations imposed on his vision by that concentration camp of the mind known as El Bronx?

Abraham Rodriguez

The female characters in Rodriguez's novels often have no one but one another to cling to for comfort—and often, even the female characters are at war with one another.

Having lived in Berlin for more than a decade, perhaps his focus is now on the ordinary people of Germany who allowed themselves to participate to the extent that they did in the Holocaust, which gave him nightmares as a child. His earliest stories were about German soldiers on the Eastern Front during World War II. Perhaps his brief biography of the Nazi propagandist Leni Riefenstahl in *South by South Bronx* is both a return to that subject and a sign of what's to come. Time will tell.

The Buddha Book: A Novel and *South by South Bronx*

If Abraham Rodriguez is to stay true to his mission as a social chronicler of the South Bronx, however, he will have to allow his subjects and themes to evolve naturally with the changing times, and he will have to learn he does not have to rely on cinematic styles at the expense of human substance. Rodriguez seems to be aware of this when he says, "A lot of my stuff has not been published. I want to show the whole Bronx, not just the crack dealers, the pimps and 14-year-old prostitutes." Why then does he use the same territory as a backdrop for a barrio noir that's packaged in well-honed cinematic techniques? In the disappointing words of the author: "It sells."

CHRONOLOGY

1961
Born in the Bronx.

1976
Drops out of Benjamin Franklin High School.

1982
Earns high school GED and enrolls at the City College of the City University of New York.

1983
Starts punk-rock band Urgent Fury with two friends from Brooklyn.

1982–1985
Wins Goodman Fund Short Story Competition twice while at City College.

1985
Drops out of college.

1990
Urgent Fury breaks up.

1991
"The Subway King" appears in *Story* magazine.

Chronology

1992
Boy Without a Flag: Tales of the South Bronx is published by Milkweed Editions. Collection includes "The Boy Without a Flag," No More War Games," "Babies," "Birthday Boy," "Short Stop," "The Lotto," and "Elba." "Roaches" appears in *Iguana Dreams: New Latino Fiction*, edited by Delia Poey and Virgil Suarez and published by Harper. *Boy Without a Flag* named in Notable Books List for 1993 by the *New York Times*.

1993
Spidertown: A Novel is published by Hyperion.

1995
Spidertown: A Novel wins American Book Award.

1997
"Baptism Under Fire" appears in Sycamore Review.

2000
"Fake Moon" appears in *Nerve.com*. "Looking for Ed Rivera" appears in *Centro*, as does "On Being Puerto Rican: Report from the Eastern Front." Wins grant for writing from the New York Foundation for the Arts.

2001
The Buddha Book: A Novel is published by Picador USA. Conducts writing workshops for the Supportive Children's Advocacy Network in Spanish Harlem.

2008
South by South Bronx is published by Akashic Books.

WORKS

Novels and Collected Short Stories

The Boy Without a Flag (1992): "The Boy Without a Flag," "No More War Games," "Babies," "Birthday Boy," "Short Stop," "The Lotto," "Elba."

Spidertown: A Novel (1993)

The Buddha Book: A Novel (2001)

South by South Bronx (2008)

Uncollected Short Stories and Essays

"Baptism Under Fire," *Sycamore Review* (winter/spring 1997)

"Fake Moon," *Nerve.com* (August, 2000)

"Looking for Ed Rivera," *Centro: Journal of the Center for Puerto Rican Studies* (Spring 2002)

"On Being Puerto Rican: Report from the Eastern Front," *Centro: Journal of the Center for Puerto Rican Studies* (2000)

"Roaches," Iguana Dreams: New Latino Fiction. Eds. V. Suarez and D. Poey (1992)

"The Subway King," *Story* (Spring 1991)

Translations

Spidertown. Dutch (1995)

Spidertown. Spanish (1999)

Spidertown. German (2000)

NOTES

Information about Abraham Rodriguez's life comes from articles he has written: "On Being Puerto Rican: Report from the Eastern Front," in *Centro: Journal of the Center for Puerto Rican Studies*, Vol. 11, No. 2 (Spring 2000): pp. 95–100; "Looking for Ed Rivera," *Centro: Journal of the Center for Puerto Rican Studies*, Vol 14, No. 1 (Spring 2002): pp. 149–153; from Allatson, Paul, "Abraham Rodriguez Jr." in *Latino and Latina Writers*, Vol. 2 (New York: Charles Scribner & Sons, 2004): pp. 971–983) and from the following interviews and articles: Hernandez, Carmen Dolores, "Abraham Rodriguez, Jr." in *Puerto Rican Voices in English: Interviews with Writers* (Westport, CT: Praeger, 1997): pp. 137–155; Rivera, Lucas, "Bronx Author Shakes up Latino Literature," *Hispanic*, Vol. 11, No. 4 (April 1998): p. 16; Minners, Jon, "The Buddha Book," *Bandwidth: A Popular Culture Electronic Magazine*, www.ybfree.com/14BUDDAH1.html (2002); Fisher, Ian, "Chronicler of Bleak Truths in South Bronx; Novelist finds His Muse Close to Home and Perhaps, Ultimately, His Escape," *New York Times*, August 9, 1993: Section B, Column 1, p. 3; Gonzalez, Carolina, "Barrio Noir," *New York Daily News*, April 30, 2008: np.

FURTHER INFORMATION

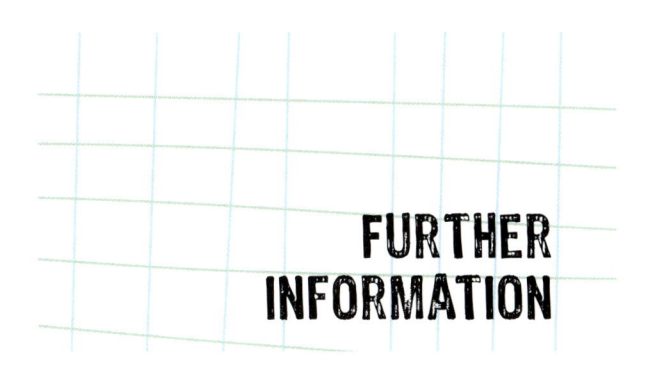

Books

This is the first young adult book on Abraham Rodriguez. For other topics, please check the bibliography.

Websites

Boricua Links
www.virtualboricua.org

National Book Foundation
www.nationalbook.org/arodriguezbio.html

Welcome to Puerto Rico
www.topuertorico.org/litera.shtml

BIBLIOGRAPHY

Acosta-Belén, Edna. *The Puerto Rican Woman*. New York: Praeger, 1979.

Allatson, Paul. "Abraham Rodriguez Jr." In *Latino and Latina Writers*, Vol. 2, 971–983. New York: Scribners, 2004.

——. "Latino Dreams: Transcultural Traffic in the U.S. National Imaginary." In *Portada Hispanica Series*, No. 14, Chapter 3, 109–153. Amsterdam: Rodopi Press, 2002.

Ashcroft, Bill, et al. *The Empire Writes Back: Theory and Practice in Post-Colonial Literatures*. New York: Routledge, 1989.

Baker, Susan S. *Understanding Mainland Puerto Rican Poverty*. Philadelphia, PA: Temple University, 2002.

Chavez, Linda. *Out of the Barrio: Toward a New Politics of Hispanic Assimilation*. New York: Basic Books, 1991.

de Noyelles, Amy. Review of *Spidertown*. *Hispanic* (March 1995): 80.

Bibliography

Dickens, Charles. *Oliver Twist*. London: R. Bentley, 1838.

Dodd, David. Review of *Spidertown*, *Library Journal* (April 1993): 127.

dos Passos, John. *The Big Money*. New York: New American Library, 1979.

Dwyer, Jim. Review of *The Boy Without a Flag: Tales of the South Bronx*, *Library Journal* (October 1992): 103.

Ermelino, Louise. Review of *Spidertown*, *People Weekly* (July 19, 1993): 27.

Feliu, Fernanco. "Esa no es mi bandera: La identidad puertorriqueña en 'The Boy Without a Flag' de Abraham Rodriguez Jr. y 'El juramento' de Rene Marques." In *Bilingual Review/ La Revista Bilingue* 24, no. 3 (Winter 1998): 230–240.

Finn, Peter. "Tenement Romance: Review of *Spidertown*." *New York Times Book Review*. July 18, 1993, 16.

Fisher, Ian. "Chronicler of Bleak Truths in South Bronx." *New York Times*. August 9, 1993, B 3.

Fitzpatrick, Joseph P. *Puerto Rican Americans: The Meaning of Migration to the Mainland*. Englewood Cliffs, NJ: Prentice Hall, 1987.

Flores, Juan. *From Bomba to Hip-Hop: Puerto Rican Culture and Latino Identity*, 43–47, 180–186, 224–225. New York: Columbia University Press, 2000.

Frick, Daniel. Review of *The Boy Without a Flag: Tales of the South Bronx*. *Studies in Short Fiction* 31, No. 4 (Fall 1994): 114.
Fuentes-Rivera, Ada. "From Home to the Crack House: Aproximaciones a la narrativa de Abraham Rodriguez, Jr." *Latino Review of Books* 3, No. 3 (Winter 1998): 28–33.

_____. "Mas alla de la estetica nuyorican y la guagua aerea: La narrativa de Abraham Rodriguez, Jr. (*The Boy Without a Flag: Tales of the South Bronx*)."*Dialogo* 6 (Winter/Spring 2001): 20–25.

Gann, L. H., and Duigan, Peter J. *The Hispanics in the United States: A History*. Boulder, CO: Westview Press, 1986.

Gonzalez, Luis Manuel. *The Economic Development of Puerto Ricio from 1898 to 1940*. Ph.D. diss., University of Florida, 1964.

Gourevitch, Philip. "Balzac of the South Bronx." *New York* (June 7, 1993): 24.

Green, John. Review of *The Buddha Book*. *Booklist* (June 1, 2001).

Greenberg, Kevin. Review of *The Buddha Book*. *Book* (July 2001): 77.

Gregory, Deborah. Review of *Spidertown*. *Essence* (November 1993): 62.

Harris, Michael. "Webs Spun of Money." *Los Angeles Times*, June 13, 1993, BR 3.

Hernandez, Carmen Dolores. "Abraham Rodriguez Jr." Interview in *Puerto Rican Voices in English: Interviews with Writers*, 137–155. Wesport, CT: Prager, 1997.

Hirsch, Diana C. Review of *The Boy Without a Flag: Tales of the South Bronx*. *School Library Journal* (January 1993): 144.

Kaganoff, Penny. Review of *The Boy Without a Flag: Tales of the South Bronx.Publishers Weekly* (May 18, 1992): 63.

Laviera, Tato. *AmeRican*. Houston: Arte Publico Press, 1988.

Lukowsky, Wes. Review of *South by South Bronx*. *Booklist* (May 15, 2008): 26.

Magill, Frank N. *Masterpieces of Latino Literature*, 1994, 46–49, 525–528. New York: Harper Collins.

Mansfeldt, Stefan. "Identity and Hybridity in Puerto Rican Fiction in English." *Zeitschrift fur Anglistik und Amerikanistik* (1999): 321–332.

Martí, José. *Selected Writings of José Martí*. New York: Noonday Press, 1954.

Minners, Jon. Review of *The Buddha Book*. *Bandwidth: A Popular Culture Electronic Magazine* (January 2002).

Mohr, Eugene. *The Nuyorican Experience: Literature of the Puerto Rican Minority*. Westport, CT: Greenwood Press, 1982.

Mohr, Nicholasa. *The Bronx Remembered: A Novella and Other Stories*. New York: Harper and Row, 1975.

Moore, Joan W., and Pachon, Harry. *Hispanics in the United States*. Englewood Cliffs, NJ: Prentice Hall, 1985.

Morales, Julio. *Puerto Rican Poverty and Migration: We Just Had to Try Elsewhere*. New York: Praeger, 1986.

Nieto, Sonia. "Fact and Fiction: Stories of Puerto Ricans in U.S. Schools." *Harvard Educational Review* 68 (Summer 1998): 133–163.

Peoples Press. *Puerto Rico: The Flame of Resistance*. San Francisco: Peoples Press, 1977.

"Picks and Pans." Review of *Spidertown*. *People Weekly* (July 19, 1993): 27.

Pietro, Pedro. *Puerto Rican Obituary*. New York: Monthly Review Press, 1973.

Pinero, Miguel. *Short Eyes*. New York: Hill & Wang, 1975.

Bibliography

Review of *The Boy Without a Flag: Tales of the South Bronx*. *Publishers Weekly* (January 1993): 144.

Review of *The Buddha Book*. *Booklist* (July 1, 2001).

Review of *The Buddha Book*. *Library Journal* (June 1, 2001).

Review of *The Buddha Book*. *Publishers Weekly* (July 2, 2001): 50.

Review of *South by South Bronx*. *Booklist* (May 15, 2008).

Review of *South by South Bronx*. *Library Journal* (May 15, 2008).

Review of *South by South Bronx*. *Publishers Weekly* (February 25, 2008): 49.

Review of *Spidertown*. *Publishers Weekly* (March 29, 1993): 33.

Review of *Spidertown*. *Publishers Weekly* (August 15, 1994): 93.

Review of Spidertown. *Tribune Books*, (July 25, 1993): 5.

Rifkind, Donna. "Uneasy Streets." *New York Times Book Review*, December 20, 1992, 717.

Rivera, Edward. *Family Installments: Memories of Growing Up Hispanic*. New York: Morrow, 1982.

Rivera, Lucas. "Bronx Author Shakes Up Latino Literature." *Hispanic* (April 1998): 16.

Rodriguez, Abraham. "Baptism Under Fire," *Sycamore Review* 9 (Winter/Spring 1997): 10–16.

_____. *The Boy Without a Flag: Tales of the South Bronx.* Minneapolis, MN: Milkweed Editions, 1992.

_____. *The Buddha Book: A Novel.* New York: Picador USA, 2001.

_____. "The Fake Moon." Nerve.com (August 22, 2000) (Website no longer available)

_____. "Looking for Ed Rivera." *Centro: Journal of the Center for Puerto Rican Studies* 14, No. 1 (Spring 2002): 149–153.

_____. "On Being Puerto Rican: Report from the Eastern Front." *Centro: Journal of the Center for Puerto Rican Studies* 11 (Spring 2000): 95–100.

_____. "Roaches." In *Iguana Dreams: New Latino Fiction.* Eds. Poey and Suarez. New York: Harper, 1992, pp. 267–285.

_____. *South by South Bronx.* New York: Akashic Books, 2008.

_____. *Spidertown: A Novel.* New York: Hyperion, 1993.

_____. "Subway King," *Story* (Spring 1991): 73–79.

Rungren, Lawrence. Review of *South by South Bronx.* *Library Journal* (May 15, 2008): 93.

Said, Edward. *Culture and Imperialism*. New York: Alfred A. Knopf, 1992.

Shorris, Earl. *Latinos: A Biography of the People*. New York: W.W. Norton, 1992.

Sondheim, Stephen. *West Side Story*. New York: Dell, 1965.

Soto, Pedro Juan. *Spiks*, ed. Rio Piedras, PR: Editorial Cultural, 1956.

Stavans, Ilan. *The Hispanic Condition*. New York: Harper-Collins, 1995.

Steinberg, Sybil S. Review of *Spidertown*. *Publishers Weekly* (March 29, 2003): 33.

Suarez, Virgil, and Poey, Delia. *Iguana Dreams: New Latino Writing*. New York: HarperCollins, 1992.

Takaki, Ronald. *A Different Mirror: A History of Multicultural America*. Boston: Little, Brown, 1993.

Thomas, Piri. *Down These Mean Streets*. New York: Knopf, 1982.

Torres-Padilla, Jose L. "Review of *From Bomba to Hip-Hop: Puerto Rican Culture and Latino Identity* by Juan Flores, and *Popular Cultures, Everyday Lives*," ed. Kelly and Radway. *Journal of Popular Culture* 36 (Summer 2002): 174–178.

Turner, Faythe. *Puerto Ricans at Home in the USA: An Anthology.* Seattle, WA: Open Hand Publishing, 1991.

Verdone, Jules. "Straddling the Criminal and Straight World. *Boston Globe* , September 19, 2001, C3.

Waggenheim, Karl, and Olga, eds. *The Puerto Ricans: A Documentary History.* Princeton, NJ: Wiener, 1999.

Wakefield, Dan. *Island in the City: The World of Spanish Harlem.* Boston: Houghton Mifflin, 1959.

Wright, Richard. *Native Son.* New York: Harper, 1940.

Zaleski, Jeff. Review of *The Buddha Book. Publishers Weekly* (July 2, 2001): 50.

INDEX

Page numbers in **boldface** are photographs.
Proper names of fictional characters are shown by (C).

Ada (C), 62, 63
Alex (C), 115, 116, 118, 119
Amelia (C), 27, 76–77,
 79–85, 88, 98, 100, 117
 interest in reading, 92, 94
 as soul mate, 102–106
American Dream, 40, 78,
 85, 99, 103
American imperialism,
 31–34, 46–47, 53, 90, 109
Andino, Victor, **30**
Angel (C), 26, 60, 61, 69, 76,
 85, 110
Anita (C), 110–113, 117
Annette (C), 61, 62, 69
Artful Dodger (C), 93, 99
Ava Reynolds (C), 115–119

Babel, Isaac, 23
"Babies," 23, 25–26, 54–57,
 65, 68–69
de Balzac, Honoré, 18, 23
"Baptism Under Fire," 73,
 106–107
Barreto, "Lefty," 18
The Big Burn, 38, **39**, **52**
Bigger Thomas (C), 94,
 95
"Birthday Boy," 26, 60–61,
 69, 76, 85, 110
"The Boy Without a Flag,"
 14, 17–18, 44–51, **48**, 70, 76,
 106, 112
 as coming-of-age story,
 49, 52–53, 57

competing worlds theme, 51
literature as social commentary theme, 49
narrator, 44
sacrifice of identity theme, 49, 52, 53–54, 57
The Boy Without a Flag: Tales of the South Bronx, 9, 25–26, **42**, 43–71, 62, 109, 110
narrative voice, 26
publication, 25–26
reviews, 65–66
Brando, Marlon, 97, **98**
Brooklyn, 23, 35, 38
Bruckner Expressway, 38, 39, 87
The Buddha Book: A Novel, 11, 17, 27, **108**, 109-113, 117

Campos, Pedro Albizu, 19, 47, **48**, 50
Catarina (C), 83-85
Cha-Cha (C), 51, 52, 53, 54
charity yielding no benefit theme, 65
classical mythology references, 59
classic writers, 18–19, 77, 93

Clint (C), 64
Colón, Cristóbal, 50
colonization, 31–34, 46, 47
Columbus, Christopher, 29, **30**
comic books, 17, 46, 62, 110, 113
coming-of-age theme, 49, 52–53, 57
competing worlds theme, 51
Cristalena (C), 27, 76, 78–85, 90, 94, 98, 100–102, 104–106, 107

Dalia (C), 57–59, 65, 69
Danny (C), 26, 59, 60, 69
David (C), 115, 116
Detective Sanchez (C), 79
in "Roaches," 61, 69, 113, 116
in *South by South Bronx*, 70, 113, 115, 116
in *Spidertown*, 70, 76, 79, 92, 94–96, 102, 105, 113, 116
Detective Shaw (C), 61, 62, 69
Diana (C), 54, 55, 57, 65, 69
Dickens, Charles, 77, 93
Dietrich, Marlene, 116, **117**

Index

Dinky (C), 110, 111, 112, 113
disaffected youth theme, 66, **67**
dominant white culture, 14, 40, 41, 49, 73–74, 76, 90, 118
Dos Passos, John, 43
Down These Mean Streets, 19, 96
dropout, 20, 23, 37, 54, 80–82, 103
dysfunctional families, 54–57, 66, 109

Edwin (C), 46, 110
"Elba," 26, 57, 59–60, 65, 69
Elba (C), 26, 57, 59–60, 65, 69

Fagin (C), 93
"Fake Moon," 62–63, 64
Firebug (C), 39, 76–77, 80–81, 87–88, 99, 100-101, 103

generation gap, 88–90
ghetto/barrio, 14–15, 27, 35, **36**, 37, **56**, 70, 83, 90, 103, 105–106, 112–113, 121

Gloria (C), 61, 69
Gooch (C), 66, 68
Grant, Cary, 119
graphic novel, 17, **108**

Hale, Edward Everett, 49
Hitchcock, Alfred, 118
Holocaust, 13–14, 97, 120

identity sacrifice theme, 49, 52–54, 57
illegal drug economy, 10, 15, 19, 21, 40–41, 78, 94, 118
  portrayed in stories, 26–28, 54–55, 57, 61–62, 69, 76, 81–83, 87–88, 97–101
  teenage boy choices and, 70
immigration, 19, **20**, 32–40, **36**, **45**, 46, 89
  generation gap and, 89, 99
  ineffectual escapism through fantasy theme, 62–63, 64

Jewish history, 13–14
Joey (C), 61, 62, 69, 85
Jose (C), 110–113
Joyboy (C), 66, 68, 85

139

Koch, Edward, 39

language, use of, 41, 43, 92
  criticism of, 23–25
  narrator language, 24–25
Latino/Latina, 90–91,
  105–106, 118
life imitating art theme,
  97–100, **98**, 107, 119
life is a lottery theme, 59
literature as social
  commentary theme, 49
"The Lotto," 26, 57–59, 65, 69
  life is a lottery theme, 59
  religion as fruitless
    theme, 58–59, 63
lotus flower reference, 59
Lourdas, Konstantin, 21, 22
lowercase people, 14–15, 76,
  92, 109
Lucy (C), 110, 111

macho codes, 100–101,
  105–106, 109,113
Maria (C), 51
Martí, José, 50
Marty (C), 63–66, 70
Melissa (C), 64
Miguel (C), 15, 18, 27, 74,
  76–80, 81–82, 84–88

life as a movie, 97–99, **98**,
  107
machoman in crisis, 100–
  102
reading, interest in, 92–96,
  95, 100
redemption, 95, 102–106
statelessness, 90–92
Mink (C), 115, 116, 119
Miss Colon (C), 46, 47, 50
Miss Marti (C), 46, 47, 50
Monk (C), 115, 116, 119
Mott Haven, 16
movies, influence of,
  97–100, **98**, 119, 121
Mr. Brownlow (C), 95
Mr. Max (C), 95
Mr. Rios (C), 46, 47, 50
Mr. Rodriguez (C), 47, 48
Mr. Sepulveda (C), 47
Myers (C), 115

Native Son, 94, **95**, 96
Nelo (C), 84, 85
Nilsa (C), 51–54, 57, 65
9/11, **114**, 115
"No More War Games,"
  51–54, 65
  coming of age theme,
    52–53

Index

identity sacrifice theme, 57
North by Northwest, 118, 119
Nuyoricans, 11, 14, 19, 22, 26, 51, 63, 96
  dialect, 23, 41
  generation gap and, 49, 89

Old Man Benitez (C), 62
Oliver Twist, 93, 99
Oliver Twist (C), 93, 94
On the Waterfront, 97, **98**
Orchard Beach, 88, 89, 99

patriarchal culture, 84, 102
Piñero, Miguel, 10, 18
Price, Richard, 23
Puerto Rican writers, 10, 18–19, 22, 41
Puerto Rico, 19, **20**
  diaspora, 32–40, **45**, 46
  early colonialism, 29–32
  language, 43
  New York experience, 9–11, 35–38, **36**
  nostalgia and, 89, 90, 99
  oppression/exploitation, 32–41, 43, 49
  stereotypes of, 74-75
  unemployment/poverty, 32
Puertorriqueños, 44

Raul (C), 62, 63
redemption theme, 95, 102–106
religion as fruitless theme, 58–59, 63
Ricky (C), 57, 58, 69
Riefenstahl, Leni, 116, 120
Ríos, Filiberto Ojeda, 50
Ritchie (C), 66–68, 85, 98, 101
Rivera, Edward, 22, 23
"Roaches," 60–62, 69, 70, 79, 85, 113,116
Rodriguez, Abraham,
  awards/acclaim, 9, 10, 22, 25
  clash of cultures, 40–41, **45**, 49
  college experience, 21, 22, 23
  criticism, 23–24
  as dropout, 20, 21, 23
  early years and influences, 15–21
  in Germany, 120
  interest in children's education, 19–20
  Jewish history, 13-14
  narrative voice, 11, 22–23, 25–27

141

novels, 9–10, 27, 28, **72**
publication, 25–28
quotes, 9, 13, 14, 28, 29, 43, 73, 109
short stories, 9, 25–26
as songwriter, 20–21, 22, 23
as voice of disenfranchised young people, **8**, 9–11, 14–15, 19, 22–23, **24**, 26, 28, 41
Rodriguez (narrator) (C), 44, 46–50, 53, 70, 110
Rosa (C), 58, 59, 63

Saint, Eva Marie, 119
Sara (C), 54, 55, 57, 69
Sartre, Jean-Paul, 94
de Sepúlveda, Juan Ginés, 50
Sexton, Anne, 116
"The Shining Star" image, 89, 90
"Short Stop," 62, 63–66, 68, 70
charity that yields no benefit theme, 65
siren reference, 59
slumlords, 34–35, 38, 87
Smiley (C), 26, 54, 55, 57
social justice themes, 119

South Bronx, 9, 13–16, 27–31, 38–41, **49**
barrios, 35, **36**
disaffective youth in, 66–71, **67**
drug economy in, 28, 60–61, 70–71, 74, 94, 99, 101, 104, 106, 109, 112
dysfunctional families, 57
as El Bronx, 10, 15, 22–23, 26–27, 41, 43, 60, 68–69, 71, 76, 88, 93, 101, 104, 106, 109, 112, 116, 118, 119
evolving condition of, 118–119
fires, 38, **39**, **52**
identity, 90–92
ways out of, 70–71, 79–80, 105
South by South Bronx, 11, 28, 79, 113–121, **114**, **117**
first person narrative, 116
third person narrative, 116
Spanglish, 24
Spanish-American War, 31–32
Spanish Harlem, 18–20, 35, 37
Spider (C),
in "Birthday Boy," 26, 60–61, 69

Index

in *Spidertown*, 27, 70, 76–81, 83, 85–88, 91–94, 96–97, 100–103, 105–106
Spidertown: A Novel, 10, 15, 18, 27–28, 39, **72**, 73–106, **80**, 109, 112, 113, 116–117, 119
  agents of change, 82–83, 102–106
  generation gap, 88–90
  identity, 90, 91, 92
  life imitating art theme, 97–100, **98**, 107
  redemption theme, 95, 102–106
  screen rights to, 28, 106
  setting, 27, 88
  structure, 11
Spook (C), 115, 116
stereotyping,
  cinematic, 117, 121
  Jewish, 13
  negative, of Puerto Ricans, 74–75, 76
  sexual, 53, 54
street gangs, 24, **24**, 37, 66
"The Subway King," 66–68, **67**, 85
sugarcane crop, 32, **33**

teenage boy choices, 70
teenage girl choices, **56**, 70–71, 83
Thomas, Piri, 10, 18, 19, 23, 96
Tolstoy, Leo, 18, 77, 93
Torres, Edwin, 18
Twain, Mark, 24, 77, 93

Urgent Fury (punk rock band), 23

Willyboy (C), 66, 68, 85
women, **120**
  as agents of change, 82–83, 102–106
  as sexual objects, 52–53, **56**, 70–71, 83, 84, 102
World War II, 10, 19, 32, 40
  Holocaust, 13–14, 97, 120
  knowledge of, **12**, 13–14, 17, 21, 120
  Puerto Rican migration, 19, **20**, 34, 89
Wright, Richard, 94, 95, **95**, 96
writing, in present time, 68

Yolanda (C), 61, 85

ABOUT THE AUTHOR

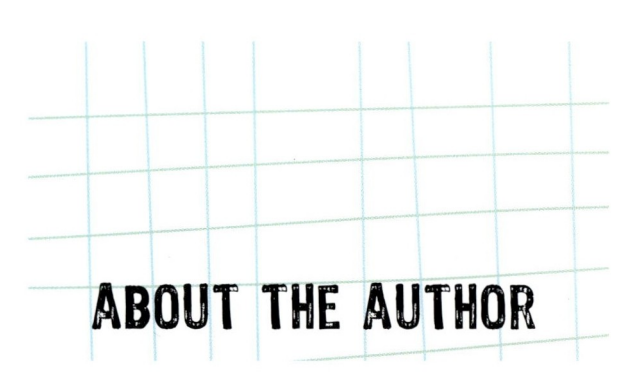

RICHARD ANDERSEN, former Fulbright Professor at the University of Bergen in Norway, Writing Fellow at Foundation Karolyi in Southern France, and James Thurber Writer in Residence at Ohio State University, currently teaches writing and literature at Springfield College in Massachusetts, where he was nominated for the Carnegie Foundation's United States Professor of the Year Award.

Dr. Andersen's twenty-five books include six on writing, five novels, seven critical studies, a children's book, a biography of Michael and Catherine Karolyi, a personal examination of contemporary education, and a book on skills for success that has been translated into three languages. For the Writers and Their Works series, he has written *Toni Morrison* and *Arthur Miller*; for the Shakespeare Explained series, *Macbeth* and *Richard III*.